W̶hat the critics are saying...

"This is a powerfully erotic and thrilling tale. Syndelle's story is the perfect follow up to SKYE'S TRAIL, the first story of the Angelini. The men are men, (when you include weres and vamps into that), and the women kick serious butt! There is a wonderfully suspenseful story here, along with the deep romantic flow of the triad's love. Even though this is a sequel, it can be read and appreciated as a stand alone. Note, this is a deeply erotic tale of three lovers and is not for the weak at heart." ~ *The Romance Reader's Connection*

"Laced with secrecy, danger and an underlying mystery, *Syndelle's Possession* takes a reader down the dark path between the insatiable bonding of three people and the all-consuming longing lying deep within their souls. The m/m/f connection intensity among the main characters defied my imagination as to what is scintillating and pushed the erotic envelope to new heights...The second book in the Angelini series does not disappoint as *Jory Strong* delivers a compelling, action-packed, and ferociously seductive tale." ~ *Just Erotic Romance Reviews*

JORY STRONG

Syndelle's THE ANGELINI
POSSESSION

ELLORA'S CAVE
ROMANTICA PUBLISHING

An Ellora's Cave Romantica Publication

www.ellorascave.com

Syndelle's Possession

ISBN # 1419953508
ALL RIGHTS RESERVED.
Syndelle's Possession Copyright© 2005 Jory Strong
Edited by Sue-Ellen Gower
Cover art by Syneca

Electronic book Publication July 2005
Trade paperback Publication February 2006

Warning:

The following material contains graphic sexual content meant for mature readers. *Syndelle's Possession* has been rated *E-rotic* by a minimum of three independent reviewers.

Ellora's Cave Publishing offers three levels of Romantica™ reading entertainment: S (S-ensuous), E (E-rotic), and X (X-treme).

S-*ensuous* love scenes are explicit and leave nothing to the imagination.

E-*rotic* love scenes are explicit, leave nothing to the imagination, and are high in volume per the overall word count. In addition, some E-rated titles might contain fantasy material that some readers find objectionable, such as bondage, submission, same sex encounters, forced seductions, etc. E-rated titles are the most graphic titles we carry; it is common, for instance, for an author to use words such as "fucking", "cock", "pussy", etc., within their work of literature.

X-*treme* titles differ from E-rated titles only in plot premise and storyline execution. Unlike E-rated titles, stories designated with the letter X tend to contain controversial subject matter not for the faint of heart.

Also by Jory Strong

Syndelle's Possession
The Angelini

ഇ

Trademarks Acknowledgement

~

Chapter One

ഇ

The wolf lurked in the shadows of Syndelle Coronado's mind, looking out into the Las Vegas night through eyes as blue as a summer sky. Magic stirred, along with the elusive promise of a mate. Or rather, two mates.

It was almost time, the magic whispered, and the wolf held that knowledge close, though anticipation rippled through it, a brush along Syndelle's spine as she turned from the hotel window and moved toward the door, unable to resist the lure of the unknown human's pain, unable to deny aid to the woman who'd somehow breached her shields and whose cry had reached her thoughts.

A trickle of fear and worry scurried through Syndelle when she stepped into the dim hallway. Only once before had she defied her parents' will and ventured out unguarded. And now she was both unguarded and alone.

But not without defenses, the wolf said, its body radiating a subtle excitement as its senses flared out, expanding to include odors and sounds that no human could experience.

Syndelle smiled, taking comfort in the wolf's presence as she always had, the fear easing, the worry remaining. She was the seventh child in her mother's Angelini bonding with a vampire and a werewolf, but she was only their second daughter. If something happened to her…the worry pressed down on her as she thought of her parents' anguish.

They'd never gotten over the kidnapping of their firstborn daughter, Jovina. And even after all of these years, not knowing what happened to their child could still bring tears to her mother's eyes and send Riesen, her werewolf mate, tearing through the forest as if he could outrun the pain, while Sabin, her mother's vampire mate, went to ground in order to avoid crossing the line from hunter to hunted—from striking out in rage and killing without the benefit of a council-ordered death sentence.

Syndelle shivered. The vampire was the ultimate predator—able to prey on both the mind and the body. So powerful that long ago they'd been banished to the night while other supernaturals had been allowed to remain in the daylight. So terrifying that the Angelini had been created to hunt them in an ancient, primitive world with few rules and where magic governed the land. And though the days of the wild magic were gone, the Angelini and their other-race mates still meted out justice, their role expanding to include not only rogue vampires, but any supernatural who broke the laws that they had all agreed upon when it came to dealing with each other and with the humans.

Syndelle smoothed a finger over the bare spot on her neck. She was the first of the ancient Coronado bloodline to forsake the tattoo of an Angelini hunter. But she was not a killer—even when the death was sanctioned and justified.

The psychic link to the girl whose physical pain called to Syndelle expanded, pushing Syndelle into motion, sending her out into the night, though she paused several blocks away from the hotel, thinking that she should have left a note for Itai, her youngest brother, and the one who was supposed to be guarding her until she could be delivered to Riesen's pack for the Howl. The wolf stirred, its body growing momentarily heavy with thoughts of the Howl, with the possibility that the Angelini magic might choose a mate from among the werewolves who would be entrusted with Syndelle's safety while Itai joined their parents and brothers.

But it was too late now. She couldn't take the time to return to the room. If the unknown woman passed out, she might not be able to locate her.

Syndelle forced the guilt away. Itai had the same heightened senses she did, though unlike her, he had also inherited the ability to shift into a wolf. He would know that no one had entered her room, and once he discovered that she was missing, he would make short work of tracking her.

She grimaced slightly. Of course, there would be hell to pay then. First from him, and then from their parents — though perhaps he wouldn't inform them. Itai was a law unto himself in so many ways — like all of the Angelini. Syndelle smiled, for once including herself as a small thrill of independence swept through her.

Her brother would probably hustle her away from Las Vegas and right into the protective custody of Riesen's old pack. That was the only reason she was here now, so that Itai could take her there. Never before had she been with one of her family members while they were hunting. But there was an unprecedented gathering of the Angelini and their parents hadn't wanted her in the presence of so many Angelini or the vampires some of them had taken for mates. It wasn't safe. There were those among the Angelini who would want her dead for what she was, for what she would ultimately mean for them.

Syndelle's heart raced along with her feet as she hurried past the rough hotels and bars, moving into a darkened industrial section, the cry of pain getting louder the closer she got, drawing her to the one she sought.

The wolf caught the scent first, slowing Syndelle so she didn't stumble over the woman who was covered in garbage — lying in it, as though she'd crawled out of the dumpster next to her. Syndelle's heart lurched at the sight. No, not a woman — a girl, only barely eighteen, if that.

Syndelle knelt and pushed the trash off the girl's naked body. The girl cringed away from her, whimpering in pain. Horror trapping the words of comfort in Syndelle's throat. Across the girl's stomach someone had carved the word *whore*. But it was the girl's face that plummeted Syndelle's heart into despair. Only vampire blood or years of treatment could ever make the face right again. It was a mass of broken bones and torn flesh.

She slipped her dark jacket off and gently covered the girl's nakedness. There were wards she could weave that would help with the pain, but in this city of dark powers, they would be a beacon drawing attention to not only the girl, but to her. Still, she hesitated, not wanting to leave the girl in the dark alley without any protection or aid. Quickly, before she could talk herself out of it, Syndelle traced a small ward over the girl. For a second it hovered, a golden pattern unseen to human eyes, and then it settled into place. "I won't be gone long. I'm going to get help."

The girl whimpered and reached for Syndelle, then cried out when her hand touched Syndelle's. A fresh wave of horror rolled through Syndelle at the sight of the distorted, twisted, broken fingers on the girl's hand.

"I'll be right back," Syndelle promised, wanting to touch the girl, to offer comfort, but afraid that if she did so, the only thing she'd bring would be more pain.

"No police. No police. Please! Go to Bangers." The girl's voice was so soft that even with her acute hearing, Syndelle strained to catch her words. "Bartender. Tell him…" The girl's cough spattered a small amount of fresh blood on an already bloody face. "Tell him. One of Daddy's girls."

"I'll be right back," Syndelle promised, her stomach aching at the thought of leaving the girl. But there was nothing else she could do.

She rose and quickly backtracked. In her mind's eye she easily pictured all of the places she'd passed. Bangers had been the last one. Uneasiness moved through Syndelle as she brought the image of the strip club into focus.

It wasn't the naked bodies that caused anxiety to curl through her like smoke. It was impossible to be related to werewolves and remain shy at the sight of flesh. It was the roughness of the crowd that made her anxious.

Restless, violent energy resonated from the men who had been trapped in the span of her memory as she'd passed Bangers. And for the first time since leaving the hotel, she welcomed the thought of encountering her brother. He hadn't shared the nature of his hunt with her, but she knew that one of the reasons he'd chosen the dark, unpleasant hotel was because it was near this group of seedy bars and strip clubs. If she encountered the prey he was seeking…

Whistles and catcalls greeted Syndelle as she approached the club. She forced a calm she didn't feel into her body. The predators who roamed here would only be more dangerous if they sensed her fear.

Even if she wasn't a lone woman entering a strip club, even if she didn't appear delicate, her sky-blue eyes a startling contrast against long raven-black hair, Syndelle knew that she would draw their attention. It was inevitable—a blessing and a curse of her heritage. She'd been created to hunt among humans, to attract and bespell them, to use them even as it was her birth-duty to guard the border between their world and hers.

Flesh of one father's flesh.

Blood of the other father's blood.

Bound together by Angelini magic to create the children who would continue the legacy.

She was one of those children.

* * * * *

As soon as Rafael Fiero saw the woman, he knew he was doomed to another night of suffering for his past sins. Fuck.

Yeah, that's what he'd do all night—until he was so desperate to come that he'd be willing to sell his soul to the devil for some relief.

Of course, there was a small problem with that. The devil wanted more than just his soul. And Rafael wasn't ready to yield—not yet anyway, though the longer he was under this particular curse the closer he came to being willing. It'd be amusing if it were happening to someone else — but it was damn painful since it was happening to him.

He brought his beer bottle to his lips and took a long drink as he imagined fucking the woman until she was limp in his arms, exhausted from being with a man who could give her orgasm after orgasm but never come himself.

His curse. His punishment.

The price he paid for his arrogance and stupidity.

Fucking vampire politics.

He took another long swallow.

But at least he had his life. Such as it was.

Rafael shifted, trying to take some of the pressure off his cock without doing something so crass as grabbing himself. Not that anyone would notice in this dark pit of a club, but he liked to think that being a vampire companion hadn't reduced him to being totally classless.

The woman made her way to the bar and his cock pulsed, pressing against the front of his jeans in rigid demand. The scent of springtime flowers reached him and for a split second he was thrown back into the past, trapped in a fleeting childhood memory of standing among green grass and bright flowers while the sun warmed him with the promise that the nightmare of his life could be held at bay.

Rafael's cock pulsed again, spilling warmth over its head and drawing him back to the present as the woman's voice reached down, stroking his balls until they were tight and hard against his body, commanding his attention until her words penetrated his consciousness.

"She begged me not to call the police. She said that I should tell you she was one of Daddy's girls."

The bartender's eyes instantly moved along the row of patrons within speaking distance and settled on Rafael. "Escort her to Big Daddy's table, Rafe, pronto."

Out of habit, Rafael's first impulse was to refuse the order. He answered only to the vampire who had made him a companion.

But there was no denying the woman's soft, pleading look, the blue eyes that made his soul want to drown in them. And when he moved closer, the springtime smell of her unleashed a primal urge to take her, to push her onto the bar and mount her. His cock pulsed, harder this time, sending another wash of wet heat over its head as his body tightened in reaction to the assault on his senses.

Chapter Two

The melody of a thousand chimes blended in perfect harmony, stealing her thoughts as Syndelle met the gaze of the one called Rafe, her vision filling with the sight of long, golden hair framing features that were as masculine as they were beautiful. Sensation and longing skittered along her nerve endings like leaves in a gentle wind, only to be followed by a rush of heat so fierce and urgent that she wanted to press up against him, to seek shelter and relief from the unfamiliar ache between her legs.

She moved closer, unable to stop herself, her hand lifting of its own accord to touch him, only to be stilled by a now familiar crush of fear and agony. The girl.

In a heartbeat, the music of the chimes faded to a hum in the background. "Please," Syndelle begged, "one of Daddy's girls is hurt. She needs help."

Rafael nodded and turned away from her, swiftly moving through the crowded bar with her in his wake. Anxiousness skittered along Syndelle's spine, a tight knot of conflicting emotion and warring desires grew in her chest, almost forcing the breath from her. She glanced at the door quickly, half expecting to see Itai. But there was no sign of him.

She touched her mind to the girl's, but found only pain and remembered terror. Rafael came to a halt next to a table of five men and without being told, Syndelle knew which one was Big Daddy. Power radiated off him, cold and ruthless, assaulting her senses with a force that was surprising for a human. When she told him about the girl, his rage and desire for revenge sent shards of pain through her skull, momentarily blocking out the gentle harmony of the chiming.

Big Daddy nodded to two of the men, his dreadlocks fanning out on either side of his face like a cobra's hood. "Take care of it."

As they rose and moved away, he waved his hand toward the now empty chairs. "Sit."

"No, I can't. I need to get back before…"

The men on either side of Big Daddy stood, prepared to enforce the command. Alarm rushed through Syndelle at the threat of violence. It would take a lot to kill her, but it was possible. And there were worse things than death.

Rafael sighed and plopped down on one of the chairs in a seemingly careless sprawl. *Shit.* He hoped this wasn't going to go badly. *Not for a fuck.*

But then again, why wouldn't it go badly this time? Going for a fuck was what had landed him in this version of hell to begin with.

May the Angelini have reason to hunt down Lilith and her whore companion, Ishana. Or at the least, let Brann be given a reason to execute them.

Rage whipped through Rafe at the memory of Lilith's trap, at the way the vampire had so casually planned on killing him in order to strike out at Brann.

Fucking vampire politics.

Even after two years of being Brann's companion, Rafe still hated them, still resented that he'd been trapped by them, forced to become Brann's companion in order to save himself. He still hated that the companion bond made it possible for Brann to know every one of his thoughts, to command him and punish him, to own him in the same way that a feudal lord once owned his wife.

In time he would have yielded to Brann, would have accepted the other man's attentions, but now he fought against the attraction. Fought against giving any more of himself than his blood — and even that he didn't do willingly.

Fucking vampire politics. But at least there was a compensation for being Brann's companion. Eventually Lilith would go too far. Eventually she would break a rule and the vampire's council would call on their executioner — Brann — to mete out her long-deserved justice. Rafe would enjoy that day immensely.

For a moment Rafael was tempted to test the link that bound him to the vampire. But for once, the deceptive-looking coin he wore around his neck was cool against his skin. Rafe smirked. *Maybe it's my night off for good behavior.* Or maybe Brann decided to stop waiting and was off fucking some other poor bastard. The thought brought a confusion of emotion that Rafael didn't want to face. He looked at the woman and said, "You might as well sit down. Big Daddy just wants to make sure it's not a trap."

The woman slowly took the chair next to his, and once again Rafe was filled with the smell of spring and the urgency to cover her body with his. Damn. He'd be lucky if he got her out of the club before he shoved his cock into her. Not that he hadn't fucked plenty of women in the sleazy private rooms that the strip club offered, but she wasn't going to be one of them.

"So what's your name?" he asked, surprising himself by the intensity of his desire to know it.

The musclemen slid back into their seats. The woman's eyes settled briefly on them, before locking with Rafael's. "Syndelle."

Big Daddy leaned back in his chair, a silent demand for attention. When Syndelle was looking at him, he steepled his fingers and studied her. "You got family in Vegas?"

"My brother."

"No sister?"

"No."

"Your eyes remind Big Daddy of his friend Skye's eyes. But you got a different feel to you than she does. You carrying?"

Syndelle's eyebrows drew together. A weapon? A baby?

His laugh reached out like a dark snake and struck her.

A weapon most likely, but the answer was the same. "No."

"Can't be related to Big Daddy's friend then. She never goes anywhere without one knife. Oftentimes more than one." He nodded slightly and the man to his right snapped his fingers. Before his hand had lowered, a bare-chested waitress in a tiny G-string was standing next to the table, replacing empty beer bottles with full ones. "Big Daddy prides himself on his hospitality. What'll you have?"

"Nothing, thank you," Syndelle said.

He shifted in his chair, and the mood at the table went cold and deadly. "You too good to drink with Big Daddy?"

"No. Another time I'd be pleased to have a drink with you. But I need to leave as soon as your men get to the girl."

As quickly as the menace had arrived, it departed. Big Daddy laughed and settled back in his chair, lifting his beer bottle in a toast. "To the Lady Syndelle."

A cell phone rang. The man to his right reached into his pocket and retrieved the phone, listening to someone but not saying anything until his attention moved to Big Daddy. "They're on their way to Doc's. Rapper says it's as bad as what happened to Tia and Angel, and looks the same."

Heavy menace settled over the table again. "Some motherfucker is going to be sorry they messed with Big Daddy's girls. Big Daddy don't let anyone ruin his merchandise." He took another pull from the beer bottle. "Tell Rapper to find Skye and take her to Doc's place so she can see this motherfucker's work up close. And after he's done with that, tell him to find Dog. Tell him to take Dog down to the tracks and find out why he wasn't watching this girl like he was supposed to be doing. Big Daddy don't like failure. Big Daddy don't like people slacking off when he tells them to do something. You tell Rapper that's the lesson he's got to teach Dog if Dog don't have a good reason for letting this happen to Big Daddy's merchandise."

The muscleman relayed the message then hung up. Big Daddy turned his attention back to Syndelle and she tensed under the stare of his cobra eyes. "You see anyone in that alley?"

"No."

His eyes narrowed. "How come a pretty piece like you was in that alley by herself? That doesn't seem right to Big Daddy. Piece like you belongs at one of the big casinos, not around here."

Syndelle groped for an answer but could think of nothing except one that contained a small measure of the truth. "I had a feeling that someone needed help."

His suspicion hung over her and once again she felt the power radiating off him, cold and ruthless, only this time dark tendrils of it moved toward her as though they would invade her soul and scare the truth from her. She stilled, surprised but not afraid. He was human with some ability—but she was Angelini.

She met his stare, watching as his pupils expanded and contracted, as he tried to wrap her in fear. Cautiously she opened herself, letting some of her own magic rise, and immediately saw the spells protecting him—dark and old with the feel of the graveyard—death magic, placed on him long ago.

His teeth flashed white and he raised his bottle, tipping it toward her in a silent salute. "You're free to go. But Big Daddy won't forget you. And he won't forget that he owes the Lady Syndelle a favor for finding one of his girls."

Syndelle nodded in acknowledgement of the pledge, then rose from her chair, with Rafael rising along with her. When she would have thanked him and escaped the strip club, hurrying back to the hotel room, he grabbed her arm and lust flashed through Syndelle—every cell in her body primed for this moment. Every cell whispering in unison. A mate!

When Syndelle tried to pull away in denial, the chiming in her mind rose in volume, making it impossible to do anything other than comply when Rafe said, "Let's get out of here," and guided her through the doors of the club and out to a car that was parked close to the building. A Viper, Syndelle noticed, the chiming lessening as he released his hold on her arm so that he could open the door for her.

Sanity returned momentarily, along with a flicker of fear. Despite the need pulsing through her body, despite the recognition of what he was to her, she didn't dare go with him. He needed to be presented to her family. She needed to know who he was, what he was. There was a hint of magic in him, a warlock's gift left fallow. She tried to move away, but before she could escape, Rafael was touching her again, crowding against her, molding his hard frame to her soft curves.

Syndelle whimpered as need coursed through her, the rampant urge to mate, to tie him to her in a primal Angelini coupling that would lock his body inside hers as she took his seed. She tried to fight it, to delay the inevitable—but the wolf and the magic that made her who she was, along with her own body, conspired against her, as though fearful that the opportunity would pass if she didn't claim it now.

Rafael fought the urge to kiss her. To strip her and press her against the hood of the car, to rut on her like a convict just getting out of prison. Despite the curse, despite the knowledge that there would be no relief for him, he was desperate to plunge his cock into her, desperate to feel her wet heat. He'd never felt this enthralled, this compelled—as though his very life hinged on joining with her.

He urged her into the car, trying to keep his touches to a minimum in order to maintain enough control to get them to the closest safe house, a bolthole that only he and Brann knew about. It was against Brann's rules, but he didn't care. What more could the vampire do to him?

Rafael's mind followed the path leading from the coin on his necklace to the vampire who had made him a companion. The way was cool and gray, blocked by a thin barrier that would yield if he were in danger, if Lilith finally decided to risk punishment, to challenge Brann directly by killing his companion. Rafael backed away, not wanting to draw Brann's attention. And within minutes he had parked the car in the garage and moved around to pull Syndelle out and through the door leading into the house.

There was none of his usual finesse, none of his usual mocking humor, there was only the desperate need for the touch of her skin, the feel of her soft and yielding beneath him. He made it as far as the wide, plush couch before lust overwhelmed him and he pushed her down on the cushions, covering her body with his as his mouth sought hers.

Syndelle whimpered under the onslaught, opening her mouth to his demanding tongue, submitting to its dominant strokes just as her cunt ached to submit to the unyielding stroke of his penis. Already she was swollen, wet, needy.

She was a virgin, guarded by her family, and yet there was no fear in her at what was to come. Her body was primed for this moment, her mind prepared. He was one of her mates. She knew it in every cell, with every breath, with the silent, insistent voice that urged her to get on her hands and knees, to display herself so that he would mount her. It was the wolf's need though she could not take the wolf's form. It was the wolf's instinct that demanded a show of submission.

She moved restlessly against Rafael, wanting the feel of skin on skin, wanting to trail kisses along his neck, his chest, to feel his heartbeat against her lips before moving down and claiming his cock. She needed to bite him, to mark him just as she needed him to mark her. It was both a vampire's craving and the Angelini magic that required a bond made strong and unbreakable by blood.

A red haze filled Rafael's mind, a hunger like nothing he'd ever experienced before, not even when the vampire grew impatient and sank his fangs into him, flooding his mind and cock with a desire from which there would be no relief—his punishment for not yielding his body to the vampire who claimed him. Rafael lifted his face and knew immense satisfaction at the sight of Syndelle's kiss-ravaged lips, at the way her chest rose and fell rapidly, the tight, hard nipples pressing urgently against her shirt.

He levered himself up further, grinding his hard cock against her jeans-covered pussy, reveling in the soft, needy sound she made, in the arch of her back as she instinctively offered more of herself to him.

With one hand he unbuttoned her shirt and spread it wide, glorying in the sight of her perfect breasts with their dark crowns. Like a starving man he lowered his head and latched onto one of her nipples, biting and sucking as he ate her responses.

She writhed underneath him, whimpering and struggling and panting, ratcheting up his hunger, feeding his need to thoroughly dominate her. His cock pulsed in time with his sucking and biting, with the hard squeezing and tugging of her other areola as his hand and fingers tormented it, with the heartbeat that thundered in his ears.

Hers. His. He wasn't sure which one he was hearing and didn't care.

Fuck, what was she doing to him? What had the vampire done to him?

He'd never known hunger like this. Never had an urge to bite as the vampire bit him, but even as he fought the compulsion, his teeth clamped down on the skin over her heart, the taste of her a heady wine that intoxicated him as he left his mark.

She sobbed and arched underneath him, her fingers moving from his hair to his back and shoulders, scratching against his shirt. Rafe growled in frustration, wanting to feel the erotic sting of her nails. But the roar in his head overrode his intention to take off his shirt, demanding instead that he strip her jeans off and bury his face between her legs.

He complied, roughly removing her shoes and shoving her jeans down and off. The scent of her arousal had him opening his own jeans and grabbing his heavy cock as his other hand clamped over her breast and his mouth zeroed in on her pussy. Her cunt lips were swollen, parted, the pink wet flesh glistening, ripe with arousal.

The savage need to plunder gripped him and he thrust his tongue into her slit, hungrily swallowing, relishing her taste and wallowing in her smell as his ears soaked up the sounds of her pleasure.

Tears streamed down Syndelle's face. Fire streaked through her blood. On some level she was aware that she was begging, her voice low and thready as she urged him to fuck her. But even as she pleaded with him, hungered for the feel of his cock thrusting in and out, invading her virgin channel, the wolf took fierce pleasure in the rub of slick, wet vulva against its mate's face, in the feel of hot tongue against sensitive flesh, preparing it further for the invasion of its mate's penis.

Syndelle's breath shuddered in and out of her body when the first wave of orgasm slammed into her, making her arch and cry out as she shoved her mound against his mouth in reaction. He brought her again with his tongue, and again when his lips clamped on her swollen clit, sucking hard and fast, a dominant male animal proving he was worthy of a mate, that he knew how to pleasure a mate.

She was weak, completely submissive after the third climax. He smoothed wet, kisses over her still-heated labia and clit before turning his face into her thigh. There was a warning nip followed by searing erotic pain as his teeth clamped down, marking her, his bite fierce enough to break the skin.

It took all of his willpower to pull away, to stand and strip out of his clothes. His cock throbbed, his balls felt swollen. He wanted to plunge into her, to rut on her wildly, but another, more primitive urge rose and he hovered over her, forcing her mouth to his neck, to the smooth spot where the vampire's fangs had so often plunged into his flesh. He cried out at the feel of her teeth, relishing the way her bite burned straight to his cock.

Of her own free will, her lips traveled downward, pausing to play with the ruby-ended barbell that pierced his left nipple.

He groaned and pressed into her mouth, enjoying her teasing licks and sucks, the way each strike of her tongue against his nipple sent a shock of ice-hot fire through his penis. His fingers tunneled through the silky strands of her midnight-colored hair, curling into fists as her mouth settled over his heart and her teeth sank in.

Every muscle in his body went taut as her lips traveled downward. His buttocks clenched and his balls pulled tight in anticipation. He cried out, body bowing, head thrown back, as her lips and tongue explored his penis, kissing, laving, sucking every hard, pulsing inch of him. He was shaking, trying to keep himself from fucking her mouth by the time she turned her face into his thigh and bit—taking his blood, taking his soul.

She slipped off the couch then, going to her hands and knees, legs spread, tempting him with a glimpse of swollen female flesh, and all thought deserted him. He was left with only the driving need to mount her, to finish claiming her.

Syndelle screamed, the pain of his rough possession, the fiery erotic agony of his huge penis forcefully opening her virgin channel made her struggle instinctively, fighting him so the wolf could offer a final test to its mate.

Virgin. The word crashed into Rafael's consciousness, but rather than gentling him, it only made the need to fill her with his cock more violent, more consuming. He couldn't stop the low foreign growl from escaping. He couldn't stop himself from pressing forward until he was fully seated in her clenching, shuddering depths. And then he clamped his teeth on the smooth skin where neck met shoulder, holding her in place, dominating her.

At the feel of his teeth, Syndelle yielded completely, lowering her head and chest so that his cock would tunnel even deeper into her body as the mating progressed. The wolf was satisfied. The wolf wanted this, needed this. And the Angelini blood that coursed through her veins would see that it ended in a permanent bond—one that linked her mind to Rafael's and ensured that her mate would forever crave her physically. One that ensured her protection so that the legacy of the Angelini would be continued into another generation of hunters.

For several long seconds Rafael savored the heady rush of domination, of knowing that for the first time in his life, his cock was the only one his partner had ever known. But then the heat of her, the low, pleading cries she was making as her channel tightened and released like a wet fist around his cock were too much to bear. He started pumping. Hard and fast. Desperate. The sensations so extreme that his groans against her shoulder sounded almost like whimpers.

He wanted to come so badly. Wanted to shoot his seed into her. Prayed that by some miracle the curse would lift and he would know the rush of fire down his spine and through his balls, the ecstasy of lava-hot semen pouring through his cock.

Frantically he pumped in and out of her wet depths, maddened each time he reached the end of her and had to pull out. Furious need drove him, a fierce desire to go even deeper, to somehow reach a place that no human woman would have.

Angelini. The word whispered through his consciousness. But her cries urged him on, demanding that he yield everything, that he slam into her with all his strength, that he push through that final barrier separating him from what he craved, what he needed to survive.

And then he was there, locked inside her body, his seed a scalding wash of pleasure as it was ripped through his cock. He shouted, instinctively fighting the tight band of muscles that locked the head of his penis into her depths, but his struggles only triggered another searing climax, and another until he was weak and spent, his face wet from the sheer pleasure he'd experienced.

Angelini.

This time the word whipped down the link between Rafael and the vampire, turning the coin around his neck into a burning coal where it lay pressed between slick, heated flesh. He jerked in reaction, as did Syndelle, then both cried out as the movement triggered one final explosive orgasm before his penis slid free and Rafael moved instantly into a sated, magic-induced sleep.

In the distance, the vampire felt Syndelle's hidden power, just as he'd tasted her ancient blood through his link with Rafael when his companion had broken the skin on her inner thigh. Now Brann's cock stood at rigid attention, his fangs ached to slide into her and he savored the sweet promise of her. He'd waited centuries to find a female such as this one. And soon she would be his for all time, bound to him by her own nature and the laws of her kind.

Chapter Three

Syndelle only barely had enough time to take a shower and put on fresh clothing before Itai arrived. He was preceded by rage and followed by the loud slamming of the hotel door. "You've got five seconds to get your ass out here, Syndelle," he yelled outside the bathroom door.

She glanced at herself in the semi-fogged mirror. Even with the shower, Rafael's scent was still on her, there would be no hiding that from her brother, but the other...the mating. Her heart thundered like a storm warning even as she tried to convince herself that Itai was like her fathers when it came to women's fashion, that he wouldn't immediately find the sleeveless turtleneck suspicious.

A sharp bang on the door made Syndelle jump. "If I have to break this fucking door down and drag you out naked, I will. Now get your ass out here!"

Syndelle took a calming breath, reminding herself that dealing with her youngest brother was the least of her problems right now. Her heart locked in her throat at the memory of the companion medallion around Rafael's neck. She hadn't recognized it for what it was until it was too late, until it burned against her skin as the vampire's power turned it into a fiery brand.

The sun would rise in a couple of hours. She'd been weakened by the mating and had only been able to use her magic to send Rafe into a light sleep, and only then because he'd been sated and willing to escape into the oblivion that she'd offered. Perhaps it would hold...standing as a barrier between her and the vampire.

A sob caught in her throat at the thought of him belonging to another woman. Why had her body betrayed her? Why had it chosen him, when the thought of sharing him with another female was intolerable to her?

She wiped her hand across her cheeks, clearing the tears from her face before taking another shuddering breath. The delay was just long enough for Itai to lose patience and rip the bathroom door open.

"What the..." Alarm filled his face at the sight of her tears and he actually took a half step back before his nostrils flared and his eyes narrowed. "You've been with a man. Did he hurt you?" The last was growled with the promise of retribution.

Yes! But Syndelle shook her head no.

"Don't protect him if he raped you." Itai grabbed her shoulders and shook her. In that moment, he looked so much like their vampire father that Syndelle couldn't help but shiver in reaction. Then, as his words penetrated, color washed over her face.

She stiffened her spine and gathered what courage she possessed into a seemingly solid wall of self-confidence. "I went with him freely."

Stormy wild-ocean eyes clashed with sky-blue ones as Itai held her gaze, attempting to force his will on her, to open her mind so that he could see her memories. She turned her head and broke the contact. "Stop it! You know that doesn't work on me!"

He shook her again before dropping his hands and stepping back. "Then you'd better have a damn good reason for leaving the hotel room."

She didn't doubt for a minute that he'd tracked her to the alley, to Bangers, and knew about the girl. "You know where I've been."

If anything, Itai's face became harsher. "Why did you go there, Syndelle?"

"I sensed her pain and I wanted to help."

"And what if it was a trap? You could have ended up like her, or worse. What good would that have done?" He made a dismissive gesture. "If you want to help the humans, then become a hunter like the rest of us. Do not waste your time on the prey, concern yourself with the predators!"

His rant was halted by the sound of someone knocking on the hotel door. Fear ripped through Syndelle as awareness washed over her. She grabbed her brother's arm. "Vampire."

He stilled, accepting what she said as true without question. "Get in the bathroom."

Syndelle shook her head. She wouldn't cower in another room while her brother fought her battles for her. "This is my fault," she said as she smoothed nervous hands over her black skirt. "I'll face it."

Itai's face hardened. "What have you done?"

The knock sounded again, firm and demanding. "There's no time to explain."

Syndelle forced calm into her thundering heart. The vampire couldn't enter without an invitation, and while she expected there to be consequences, that the vampire had sought her out and not simply waited and attacked made Syndelle hope for…no, not hope. Resolution replaced the threatening despair. There had to be a way to break the Angelini bond, even if it meant she would suffer for it, even if it meant that she would never mate again. She would not share with another female.

Syndelle took a step forward, prepared to open the door, but Itai grabbed her and thrust her behind him. In three steps he had the door open. She heard Rafael say, "Oh fuck," before another male voice poured through her like warm honey. "I am Brann O'Ciardha. Your sister has claimed my companion as her mate. Do you invite me in so that we can handle this matter?"

Itai stiffened as though he'd been struck. Turning, his eyes went to Syndelle's face and then to the black turtleneck. His voice was harsh and demanding as he growled, "Syndelle?"

She nodded and felt the hot energy of his werewolf blood colliding with the cold power of their vampire heritage, forming a furious storm in the small confines of the room. "I don't fucking believe this! What the fuck were you thinking of, Syndelle! What the fuck am I going to tell Mom? Not to mention Sabin and Riesen?"

Syndelle moved back, seeing Brann for the first time. Deep inside her, Sabin's memories stirred in the presence of this vampire. But she didn't take the time to search for them.

The melody of a thousand chimes, a dark song of power and emotion, whispered through her mind, leaving no doubt that this vampire whose hair made her think of a waterfall of blood was her second mate.

Fear of the vampire warred with relief — that Rafe was not claimed by another female — and mixed with curiosity as to how Rafael had ended up with Brann. She forced her gaze away from the vampire's and sought her brother's. Her mouth was dry, but she made herself say the words, "I give my permission for him to enter."

Itai stepped aside as the vampire moved into the tiny hotel room and stopped in front of Syndelle, with Rafael halting next to him. Her nipples went to tight points, her well-used channel spasmed with need as the scent of Rafael and their earlier mating surrounded her.

The presence of the vampire had her heart roaring in her ears so loudly that she knew Brann and Itai would hear it, that both would have to clamp down on their predatory instincts, would have to force themselves to remember that she was not prey.

"What the fuck have you done?" Itai growled again, his wolf's instinct reacting to her pounding heart with the need to hunt, while his Angelini blood demanded that he mete out justice to this vampire who would dare to threaten his sister in any way.

The vampire's eyes moved along Syndelle's body and she shivered at the look of possessiveness in them. "Do you acknowledge the claim, Syndelle? Or do I force you to strip so that your brother will see the marks that my companion made when you took him as your mate? Do I have Rafael do the same, baring the marks you made on his body?"

When she hesitated, Itai reached for her, as though he would force her to deny the claim, but before his fingers could curl around her arm and shake the truth from her, Brann moved between them, his presence a barrier. "By law she is mine to punish as I will, even unto death. The bond between a vampire and their chosen companion is more sacred even than the bond between a vampire and the fledglings he sires."

Itai's nostrils flared. "Vampire law does not apply here. This is a matter for the Angelini."

Brann's smile was predatory, confident, triumphant, as he turned slightly so that he could include Syndelle in his gaze. "Then I will claim her under the custom and rules governing your race. Ask your sister what I am to her."

"Syndelle?" Itai asked, dread forming on his face as he read the answer in her eyes.

Honor required that she answer truthfully. Her words were whisper-soft, but with his wolf's hearing they were a shout that made Itai cringe in anticipation of their parents' reaction. "He is my other mate."

Chapter Four

Fear skittered along Syndelle's nerve endings as the Viper pulled away from the hotel. She could feel Brann's immense power moving against her own like a hungry tiger rubbing its face and body against the bars of a cage—only it was the prey trapped inside the cage and not the deadly predator.

Her blood sang with Sabin's ancient knowledge of who Brann was, what he was.

Sorcerer. Executioner. Vampire. A being who would recognize what she was, a being who could unleash the ancient magic inside her and use it for his own purposes.

The mate of her nightmares. The bogeyman she'd feared her entire life.

But even so, the melody of a thousand chimes sang in her mind, insisting that she finish what she started, that the bond be closed. The feel of Rafael's hard cock against her bottom as he held her on his lap in the tight confines of the sports car, adding to the need.

She pressed her forehead against the window and closed her eyes, trying to block out the sound of the chiming, the urgent, primordial call to merge with these two men.

That she would ultimately yield her body was a foregone conclusion. She knew it, accepted it. Only death would free her from the demands of the Angelini magic that had created her, and she had no death wish.

The call to mate with Rafael had overwhelmed her, surprised her, pleased her. He was human and she did not fear humans. He was what she'd once hoped for, a human mate.

Like a turtle, she pulled deeper into her shell, retreating to a place where neither the chiming, nor the heady scent of Rafael, nor Brann's power could reach her, retreating to a place where she could pull her strength and courage around her.

Syndelle. Already the name resonated within Brann, calling to his body, his soul, his heart.

She was a prize beyond measure, beyond compare, one he'd thought might be more vampire myth than reality.

The Coronado family had guarded her and kept her secret well. So well that there was not even a whisper among members of the council of her existence, of what she was, what she would be to the vampire who could possess her. He doubted that even the Angelini knew what she was. There would be those among them who would want to see her dead if they knew, who would fear the return of the old magic, the old days, should she fulfill the destiny carried within her blood.

Brann pressed against her shields again, harder this time, using his link with Rafael to try and move into her mind. The way was blocked. Impenetrable.

Only the most ancient, the most powerful vampires had shields so strong. But he would have expected nothing less from Sabin's daughter. He would have expected nothing less of the Coronado line. Or from *The Masada*.

He pushed again, trying to gauge whether his attempts to breach her barriers were weakening her, but felt only the flare of her power countering his own. They were well-matched, a perfect complement to one another.

Brann smiled in the dark interior of the car. The battle would be delicate, though hard-fought, but in the end his will would reign. In the end, she would be the answer to his centuries' old prayer, one that had started the first night he awakened as a vampire. In the end, she would be his companion—bound to him by blood, his in every way, his to command even as it was his duty to protect and provide for her.

Rafael shifted in his seat, his cock so hard and full that he felt more animal than man. A multitude of feelings and conflicting desires warred along his nerve endings and down his spine. Brann's powerful will pressed through his veins, adding to the tangle of emotion and sensation swirling inside Rafael until he couldn't stand it anymore. "Enough already. Get out of my fucking head!"

His harsh snarl made Syndelle tense on his lap, the involuntary clench of her buttocks sending a shockwave through his penis. Rafe's arms tightened around her, forcing her body down hard on his erection. Fuck, after years of not being allowed to come, he was about a breath away from shooting his load into his own pants. "Don't move," he growled against Syndelle's neck, his teeth automatically clamping down on the place where he'd bitten her earlier.

She whimpered in response, her body going soft and submissive, and Rafael knew he'd be lucky to make it out of the car before taking her again. He groaned against her spring-scented flesh, his heart racing as the Viper moved through the wrought iron gates of Brann's most heavily protected home. A thin layer of sweat coated his body as he fought off the need to rut like a crazed wolf.

Brann's anticipation stroked along their link and he knew the vampire wanted this. Wanted to see him fucking her. Wanted much, much more than just that.

Rafael didn't know which was worse—what the vampire's bond had done to him or what the Angelini mating had done to him.

He was panting by the time the car came to a stop.

Rafael's harsh challenge to the vampire had jolted Syndelle out of her protective shell and into a maelstrom of emotion and desire. There was no fighting the need to mate. Rafael's cock burned through their clothing, his heavy breathing and the feel of his teeth awakened the wolf and the Angelini magic rose with it.

Brann got out of the car and moved to the passenger side, opening the door and easily lifting Syndelle from Rafael's lap. It was the first time he'd touched her and a whimper escaped as the dark melody of his power poured through her and the wolf lifted its head, howling, its song blending with the music of a thousand chimes. She shivered, resting her head against the waterfall of Brann's hair, its deep red color a reminder of what was to come. She wouldn't escape this night without exchanging blood with him. He would never allow it.

They moved through the house, so quickly that Syndelle was left with only vague impressions of rich colors and priceless artifacts. Brann stopped in a room with no windows, though Syndelle could still feel how close the sun was to rising.

Rafael joined them, reaching for Syndelle as Brann lowered her to her feet, his need was a furnace blast across her senses and Syndelle offered no resistance as Rafael's hands roughly stripped her of her clothing. She could do nothing but yield as he fell to his knees, rubbing his face in the soft down of her pubic hair before forcing her legs apart and driving his tongue through her flooded, swollen slit.

Syndelle cried out, her back arching, her face lifting as the wolf's face lifted to howl its pleasure. Brann's hands covered her breasts then, pulling her back to his now bare chest, holding her there, imprinting his heat and scent on her.

"We will mate, Syndelle, and you *will* become my companion," he purred, letting her feel the brush of his fangs against her neck as his fingers squeezed her nipples, demonstrating how much her body wanted his. She cried out, unable to do anything other than push into his palms as his possessive touch burned like a hot wire from her areolas to her clit.

Rafael growled against her wet pussy, claiming her attention and making her go weak as he took her swollen knob into his mouth, torturing her by striking the sensitive bud with his tongue, by swirling over and around it, and then by sucking hard and fast, his continuous moans and wet sucks washing over her, sending the wolf into a frenzy that wouldn't be eased until it was mounted.

She thrashed against Brann's body, crying out, alternating between trying to escape the extreme pleasure and trying to thrust her clit deeper into Raphael's mouth. Their hold on her was ruthless, forcing her to stay still, to endure until she was panting, pleading, sobbing for release.

With a deep growl, Rafael shoved his fingers into her cunt, going unerringly to her most sensitive spot and stroking as his tongue and lips feverishly worked her clit, sending a convulsive, scalding wave of orgasm through her just as Brann sank his fangs into her neck.

Oblivion threatened, a dark wave of exquisite pleasure as climax slammed through her, opening her senses, lowering her shields so that the hot magic of her Angelini blood collided with Brann's ancient vampire power as he took her blood, drinking of her essence in deadly, seductive pulls, and forging a link between them.

Rafael's teeth stung her thigh as he clamped down on the mark he'd left during their first mating and an erotic current whipped from Rafael's bite to the place where Brann's teeth pierced her skin. Syndelle screamed, thrashing wildly, instinctively fighting against a pleasure so extreme that it threatened to annihilate all her defenses and leave her completely helpless. Their hold on her tightened as the white-hot shocks of ecstasy escalated until the only escape was to yield to her body's demands and let the tidal wave of release roll over her, spinning her and sucking her under, embracing her, until finally stilling and cradling her in its dark depths.

Rafael's hand went to his jeans, unzipping the fly and pushing them down, freeing his cock and gripping it tightly to keep from coming. He'd only been able to last this long because of the companion bond, because Brann's *will*, his command made it possible.

Fierce masculine satisfaction surged through Rafe at the sight of Syndelle passed out from the pleasure, but he prayed her faint wouldn't last. He was desperate enough to rut on her unconscious form.

She stirred and Rafael eased back on his heels, watching as Brann pulled away from Syndelle's neck, his fangs slowly retracting. Syndelle's eyes fluttered open and a wash of embarrassed color flooded her face, unexpectedly filling Rafael with tenderness.

Brann's voice stirred in Rafael's mind. *The sunrise grows closer. Put her on her hands and knees and mount her.*

The command chased away Rafael's softer emotion. He grasped Syndelle's hips and eased her down, settling her on her hands and knees as Brann freed his own penis, taking it in hand. Rafael tried to look away from the sight of Brann stroking his own cock, but he was trapped, the bond between them making it impossible to escape the knowledge of what Brann ultimately wanted from *both* his companions. Of what Brann wanted *him* to willingly offer and accept. What he had not yet succeeded in getting from Rafael.

But there was no refusing the command to mount her. He *would* fuck her. He would take her while Brann watched and he would know just how much the vampire enjoyed it.

Animal instinct took over, Angelini magic and vampire compulsion, and Rafael could do nothing but cover her body with his, mounting her and thrusting his penis into her in one fierce stroke that had her lifting her head, crying out.

Brann joined them on the floor, one hand on his shaft while the fingers of the other speared into Syndelle's hair and guided her mouth to his hungry cock.

She whimpered, fighting Brann's silent command, her sheath tightening in reaction and sending unbearable pleasure through Rafael's penis. He groaned and thrust faster, harder, his teeth automatically sinking into the place where Brann had taken her blood.

Syndelle submitted instantly, burying her face in Brann's groin, licking and sucking, her moans adding to the frenzy that Rafael felt. He pounded in and out of her, suddenly desperate to reach the deep ring of muscles that would clamp down on the head of his cock and lock him to her body.

Sweat poured off him, his breath heaved in and out of his chest in panting groans. She shifted so that he went deeper and lust roared through him like a freight train. He clamped down harder on her tender skin, tasting her blood, hearing its call.

She shivered and whimpered and he felt the last deep barrier yield in the instant before she trapped him in her body, triggering one orgasm after another for all three of them.

When it was done, Rafael only barely had enough energy to roll off her. His hand moving to her hip, intending to pull her down and cuddle her against him in contented sleep.

No. Brann's sharp command brought Rafe's attention to where Syndelle's face was still buried in the vampire's groin. He couldn't look away as Brann eased Syndelle's mouth from his cock and held her lips against his inner thigh.

"Finish it, Syndelle," Brann ordered and along the Angelini bond that Rafael shared with her, he felt something dark and primordial stir in anticipation as Syndelle obeyed, clamping down on the offered flesh, giving Brann the first mating mark.

Rafael felt the vampire's satisfaction. It washed over him along with the knowledge that Syndelle's taking of Brann's blood was almost as pleasurable to the vampire as the taking of his seed.

Chapter Five

&

The wolf stirred in the early afternoon sunshine, satisfied with the claiming of one mate and the taste of the other. Now a different type of hunger moved through its body. The growl in its belly echoed in Syndelle's stomach and she groaned, rolling to her back on the soft bed, her body arching, stretching, as both she and the wolf enjoyed the feel of muscles sliding smoothly under skin.

She lay with her eyes closed, wanting to enjoy the warmth of the sun before she got up and went to find something to eat. The wolf settled, allowing her a few moments, its contentment rolling through her in gentle waves.

I hope you know what you've done, she told it, shivering as her mind ranged back to the previous night and Brann's promise to make her his companion.

The wolf lifted its muzzle, drawing Rafe's scent deep into its lungs and sending a pulse of heat through Syndelle's body, making her cunt swell and grow wet so that she clamped her legs together in reaction.

The wolf relented.

Slipping inside herself, Syndelle curled her arms around the wolf and buried her face in its warm, comforting fur. Though her wolf was forever trapped inside her because Syndelle couldn't take its form, it was as real to her as those that resided in her brothers, as those that resided in the pure werewolf females who could shift.

The wolf was always with Syndelle, though sometimes it faded, watching and waiting from the shadows as ancient magic whispered in Syndelle's ears, guiding them both toward an unwanted destiny. She shivered as her thoughts moved to Brann. Few vampires dabbled in magic for fear of altering or destroying the very force that reanimated them and allowed them to live.

Brann was the exception.

A sorcerer. An executioner. A vampire.

She shivered again as her vampire father's memories stirred, trying to rise from deep within Syndelle's mind. The blood link between Sabin and her more complex than between most vampires and their Angelini offspring.

The nightmare of losing their first daughter had never left her parents. When Syndelle was born, they'd tried to further protect her by giving her Sabin's blood along with her mother's milk. His blood had changed her, set her apart, perhaps opened the door so the ancient magic could reach her and shape her into its vessel. She shivered, remembering the exact moment her family had discovered what she was.

Syndelle gave the wolf another hug, her attention shifting outward, avoiding the memories and the fear that would come with them. The sun was up. And though she could feel Brann's presence hovering in the distance, he was not her mate yet and she was not his companion. Her shields were strong enough to easily block him.

She opened her eyes and studied her surroundings. This was obviously Rafe's bedroom. His clothes where scattered on the furniture in casual disregard of the closet that stood open. Magazines lay in small stacks. Hot rods. Computers. Video gaming. She smiled and rolled off the bed, suddenly anxious to shower, to eat, to find Rafael.

She found him in the room they'd been in the night before. The room with no windows, the only one in the house beside his bedroom and the kitchen, that had been designed for comfort and wasn't filled with priceless artifacts and antiques. He was sprawled on a chair in front of a huge screen, his hands quickly manipulating the controls of a video game. He glanced up briefly, his eyes moving over the thin tank top and jeans, a mocking smile playing over his lips before his attention returned to the screen. "If you need a fuck, you're going to have to wait 'til I get done with this mission."

His words slapped her and the spark of pleasure she'd experienced at finding him, died in her chest. The unexpected assault struck at her very core, sending an unfamiliar wash of loneliness through her. She turned, thinking to retreat, to explore Brann's home and grounds. "Not like you guys to turn tail and run," Rafe said, his words halting her in her tracks.

Syndelle stood with her back to him. It would require almost no effort at all to open the mental link between them and read his thoughts so that she could understand his unkind words, and match them to the confusing swirl of emotions she felt in him. But she did not want to take what he didn't willingly give.

"What do you know of the Angelini?" she said, remaining where she was, delaying the moment when she would have to decide whether to stay or go.

Silence stretched between them. She could feel his brief flash of confusion as his mind lightly skimmed the barrier that blocked his thoughts from her, the link with the vampire making Rafael aware in a way another human wouldn't have been.

The turbulent flow of emotion around him calmed and he sighed heavily. She could hear him drop the game controller and rise to his feet. He moved toward her, not stopping until he was so close that his scent and body heat surrounded her.

He filled her senses. He was her mate. Her husband, and yet she knew nothing about him other than the fact that he was bound to an ancient vampire.

Rafe grabbed her arm and turned her to face him. The wolf uncurled, stretching and shaking itself as its attention roamed over the taut, heavily aroused male in front of it.

"What do I know of the Angelini?" Rafe growled and the wolf actually licked its lips. "I know that before you came along I was just screwed—" his mouth twisted, "—though not by Brann, at least not yet, if that's what you're wondering. But now I'm royally fucked. Completely and totally fucked." His hands went to the waistband of her jeans. "So I might as well enjoy the perks of being able to come again, because that was a real bitch, night after night of fucking my brains out and never being able to get off."

Syndelle hesitated for only a second before grabbing his wrists and stopping him from opening her jeans. The wolf tested her will, then shook itself again and retreated, its low voice grumbling as it moved out of her consciousness. It wanted him. It would take him without regard to what he thought or what emotions swirled within him. It cared only that his cock was full and his testicles were heavy with seed. But Syndelle wanted more from Rafe. Last night she'd been helpless against her Angelini blood and the wolf's instinct to take a mate, but today they didn't rule her. She pushed at his hands, relieved when he yielded.

He studied her intently and she licked her lips nervously, wanting to spend time with him but not wanting to feel the bite of his sharp words. "Would you show me around the house?" she finally asked.

Rafael's surprise moved down their bond, forming a tentative truce between them. He shrugged, casting a quick glance at the paused video game before saying, "Sure, why not. That mission's a total washout. I've already been gutted twice and gunned down once."

Syndelle laughed, not letting his words sting. "You sound like Itai. He's got a collection of video games. Our parents have to hide them from him when they want to send him on an errand or get his help on a chore he dislikes." Feeling Rafe's surprise deepen, she added, "The Angelini do not keep blood-bound servants as the vampires do, and my parents are cautious about who they allow into our home. That and Riesen's strong

43

Were blood have made us a close family. We take care of what needs to be done without bringing in outsiders."

Rafe's surprise edged into puzzlement and Syndelle could feel the pulse of a command sharply given along the link between him and Brann. Rafael's lips curved into a challenging smile, the dare directed at their unseen companion, as he said, "If you're such a close family, how come you don't claim Skye as your sister? How come you didn't run to her and have Gian intercede when you found out you'd just mated yourself to a vampire's companion?" Now his smile returned to the mocking one she'd seen earlier, the one she already hated. "Not that it would do any good. You do know that your sister's mate is Brann's creation? That Brann is his sire, right?"

Before the words had even finished leaving his mouth, Rafe tensed and she could sense the vampire's painful rebuke rushing through Rafael's body. Without thought to what it might mean, to what it would reveal, her own link to Rafael strengthened, dropping a heavy shield between him and Brann.

Syndelle's heart thundered in her chest and she braced herself for the vampire's wrath at daring to interfere between him and his companion. But instead of anger vibrating against her shields, she found only the purr of satisfaction and anticipation.

A fresh jolt of fear raced through her as she recognized Brann's cunning. He'd wanted to know how strong her bond with Rafael was, and now he knew. For the moment, Rafael was more hers than his.

Syndelle shivered as Brann's power rubbed sensuously against hers, communicating without words his intent. In the end, both Rafael and she would belong to him—totally, completely, in every way—bound together by both Angelini magic and vampire companion bond.

Deep inside her the wolf stirred, testing the air for a danger it could help her fight. When it didn't find one, it brushed its head against her soul in a soothing, calming gesture that stroked her confidence and automatically slowed the frantic pace of her heart. *Only a mate as powerful as this one can keep us safe. But he will not crush our will. He doesn't truly understand what it is to be bound to us. Once he is our mate, he will crave us as desperately as we crave him, and he will soon understand that we are his equal. He thinks that a vampire's companion bond will give him control of us as it would with a human, that we will bend to his commands, yielding everything to him. He will learn soon enough that he is wrong.*

Syndelle took a deep, calming breath and forced her attention away from Brann. For a split second she felt his amusement, and then like the wolf, the connection faded, becoming only the barest flicker of light in a pitch-dark universe.

"Nice trick," Rafe said, "you'll have to teach it to me."

Syndelle reached up, freeing the companion medallion from underneath Rafe's black muscle shirt. Like the night before, it was cool to the touch, innocuous, though now that she was studying it closely, she recognized some of the ancient symbols and saw it for what it was.

Her mother wore Sabin's companion medallion, though any who looked at it knew instantly what it was and what it meant, unlike this ancient coin-like disc that Rafe wore. She smoothed her thumb over the surface, opening her inner vision so that she could take its full measure. "How did you end up with him?"

"Wrong place at the wrong time, and fucking the wrong woman." The mocking smile returned. "Story of my life."

She dropped the medallion and stepped back, her nerves raw from dealing with her two mates. But she wasn't ready to escape from Rafael yet.

Her thoughts returned to Rafe's comment before Brann had made his presence known. The conversation with Big Daddy played out in her memory. "Why do you think this woman, Skye, is my sister?"

Rafael's eyebrows rose. "Other than the fact that she could be your brother's twin? Let's see, she's Angelini but she doesn't wear a tattoo on her neck. I've only met two hunters like that—

you and her. You guys forming a rebellion? Not that I mind. Fucking women with tattoos on their necks isn't a real turn-on for me. And some of the Angelini tattoos are enough to cause nightmares. 'Course, those just might be leftover vampire terrors."

"Where would I find this woman?"

"Sometimes at a place called Fangs. Gian co-owns it."

In the distance, she could feel Brann's attention sharpen, so she backed off, changing the direction of her thoughts. "The one called Big Daddy ordered his men to take Skye to the injured girl. Is she a healer?"

Rafe snorted. "Only if you consider putting someone out of their misery — permanently — a form of healing."

Syndelle remembered the relayed conversation between Big Daddy and one of the other men. "There have been other girls like the one last night?"

"Two that I've heard of."

"Skye is hunting for the one who injured them?"

Rafe shrugged. "That's Big Daddy's business, and hers. Not mine."

"But you know him and you were at Bangers, when you could have been anywhere else."

For the first time his face tightened. "I was there because Brann ordered me to be there."

"Why?"

"Who the hell knows with vampires?" The mocking smile reappeared. "And what the fuck do I care? The women there are easy and there are plenty of private dance rooms for screwing your brains out. It's as good a place as any."

His words drove her backward a step, as he'd intended them to. The temptation to open the link and know his thoughts, to read his memories and understand him through them was almost unbearable.

She moved away from temptation, out into the hallway where the sun's light bathed her in its brightness. Where its touch strengthened her shields.

The previous night had spun out of control the moment she'd seen Rafael. The demands of the wolf and the chiming Angelini song had made it impossible to think beyond securing her mate. But now she could look back, examine the strangeness of being drawn by a human's pain, relive the mix of nervousness and excitement along with the small thrill of independence she'd experienced at finally facing the challenge of going out by herself.

Her heart raced with fresh excitement. Possibilities swirled inside her like leaves picked up and twirled by the wind before being dropped on the floor of the forest to form a pattern.

The girl was central to the design.

Because of her, Syndelle had been drawn to her mates...and perhaps to the lost sister her parents still mourned. Because of the girl, Syndelle had gotten her first taste of freedom, her first chance to use her own skills in some small way to help someone other than her family.

Syndelle's heart danced in nervous anticipation. She was not a hunter, but she could aid Skye in finding the monster that had left the girl broken and scarred. And in the process she could get to know this woman who was probably her sister. *Jovina, daughter of the sky.* Her parents rarely spoke the name, but it whispered through Syndelle now. She would know immediately if Skye was her sister. Blood knows blood, more so for Syndelle because of the link she shared with Sabin.

She looked at Rafael again and found him lounging in the doorway. Even the insolence radiating off him did not stop her body from reacting to him—to the sight of his long blond hair pulled back in a ponytail, the muscle shirt stretched tight, showing off his upper body, the faded jeans emphasizing his huge cock.

The mocking smile appeared. His hand moved down to cup himself through the fabric of his jeans. "Ready for stud service?"

His words pierced her, but the pain she felt wasn't hers, it was his. Between one heartbeat and the next, the window of his soul cleared just enough for her to see the desperate path he'd lived—where sex was a shield, a weapon, a survival skill, an attempt to fill a deep, seemingly endless void.

She moved into him, close enough so that their breath and heat mingled, but not so close that their bodies touched. "I won't use you that way, Rafe."

He laughed, a harsh bark of unhappiness. "That's an easy promise for you to make." He leaned in so their cheeks brushed against each other. "You're not a guy, so you don't know what it's like to fuck all night, to fuck your partner through one screaming orgasm after another and not be able to come yourself. That was one of Brann's little punishments for having to make me his companion in order to save my life." Rafael's tongue stroked her earlobe and sent a shiver through Syndelle. "But now you're here and his curse doesn't work between us. So all you have to do is walk in the room and I want to ram my cock into you hard and fast, over and over again until my balls explode and my dick screams from coming inside you."

He pulled back, his gaze meeting hers, his lips curling up in a faintly mocking smile that didn't reach his eyes. "So when we fuck, you'll just have to figure out who's using and who's being used. But I'm not going to waste time worrying about it."

For a long moment she held his gaze, his words ricocheting around inside her like a bullet intent on doing maximum damage. If he were an unbound human without a blood-tie to a vampire, a blood-tie that she shared, it might have been possible to break the Angelini bond. But not now. She knew it without seeking counsel. The truth of it whispered into her mind on an ancient voice.

Tears threatened and she turned away, feeling heartsick and lonely. The wolf rose from the shadows then, moving to stretch and bask in the sunshine, drawing the sun's warmth into both of them. And once again Syndelle's attention returned to the girl she'd found in the alley and to the woman who might be her sister.

She would seek Skye out on her own if she had to, but it would be foolish to make that her first choice. "Will you take me to Fangs?"

Along the bond, Brann's command flared to encompass both Rafael and her. *You will not leave the safety of the house and grounds.*

"The club's not open until the sun sets. I doubt you'd find Skye there before then," Rafe said.

She turned to face him again. "Do you know where they'll take the girl?"

He shrugged. "Most of Big Daddy's low-end girls stay in a house down by the railroad tracks and the biker bar."

"Will you take me?"

Rafe's lips quirked upward as Brann's command not to leave whipped through them both again. "Sure, if you can get us out of here."

He moved past her then, leading her down the hallway and to the garage. The blood-red Viper gleamed in the dusky darkness. Next to it was a black Boxster.

Syndelle smiled at the sight of the cars. All of her brothers owned flashy sports cars like these. Only her parents chose to drive vehicles that didn't call attention to themselves.

Rafe indicated the Porsche and moved around to the driver's side. She climbed into the passenger seat, her excitement building as the engine roared to life and the garage door swung open.

They backed out and swung around on the circular driveway, stopping only when they came to a keypad several feet away from the wrought iron gates blocking their path.

"The gate only stays open for a few minutes," Rafe said, making no move to key in the code. "This is as far as I can go right now."

Syndelle could feel the wards protecting the house and gardens. For the most part they served to keep others out, but one had been crafted to keep them both inside. She studied it with her mind's eye, seeing the delicate weave of intricate symbols as clearly as if they were written on paper.

Next to her, Rafe gritted his teeth and tilted his head backward. "Any time now would be good. And while you're at it, if you want a tour guide, you need to get him out of my fucking head again."

Out in the sunshine Brann's commands were easy for her to block, their blood-link not strong enough to break through the barriers created by her training, her magic, and the rich flow of Sabin's ancient blood that coursed through her veins. With a thought, she extended her protection to Rafael and was rewarded by the sound of his laugh.

She turned at the sound, her heart jolting with pleasure at the expression on his face, at the infectious smile he was directing at her. "Nice work. Take care of the rest of it and we can blow this joint."

Syndelle wrinkled her nose at his bad imitation of an old-time gangster and his smile widened. He leaned over and covered her lips with his, giving her a brief, playful kiss, before saying, "Let's give him a run for his money."

For a moment she hesitated, heart pounding with excitement and trepidation. Did she dare defy Brann? Did she truly dare to venture out?

The wolf looked up then, pulling back its lips, the flash of sharp canines a startling contrast to the gleam in its eyes. *Let him pursue us, let him fight to win us, let him prove his worth to us by showing his strength and dominance.*

Syndelle turned back toward the gate, and with her pulse racing and dancing, she lifted her hands, her fingers signing gracefully as she unraveled the complicated, powerful ward until finally it popped against her senses.

Rafe laughed again and punched the keys on the alarm pad. Within seconds, the gate swung open and they were free.

Chapter Six

Syndelle recognized the men lounging with relaxed menace in front of the house. They'd both been at the table with Big Daddy. "Will he be here?" she asked as she and Rafe moved toward the porch where the men waited.

Rafael shrugged. "Don't know. Big Daddy isn't on my list of people to keep track of."

Something in his tone made her ask, "But there are people that Brann has you watch?"

"You don't think he keeps me around just for my looks, do you?"

The mocking tone was back, but there was something else as well. She slowed her steps, wanting to prolong the moment, wanting to better understand the relationship between her two mates. "He takes your blood."

Rafael's steps slowed, too. He shot her a look, his smile both mocking and challenging. "And he wants everything else that goes with it...you do know that, right? Brann goes both ways and he's powerful enough to have two companions to satisfy his...assorted cravings."

Despite Rafael's sarcastic tone and the expression on his face, Syndelle could feel his tension along their link. She shrugged. "Among the Angelini, it is not uncommon for all the individuals in the bond to be lovers."

Surprise showed briefly on Rafe's face and flared along their connection, though his response was one she'd almost come to expect, one she was beginning to see as part of his complicated way of defending himself against being hurt. "So because your fathers fuck each other and your mother, you figured your mates would end up doing it, too."

Even anticipating Rafe's response, she couldn't keep the fire from racing across her cheeks. Sex and nakedness were not taboo in the Coronado household...nor were the sounds and scents of passion easy to mask around children with both vampire and wolf blood flowing through their veins. Still, she preferred not to think of her parents in that manner...and the image of Sabin and Riesen coupling was... Syndelle shook the thought aside before it could take hold. "No, it's not like that in my parents' bond, but is *obviously* that way among some."

A mix of emotions crowded the link between them, but there was no time for further conversation. Even moving slowly, they'd drawn near to the house and Big Daddy was stepping out onto the porch.

"Well, this is a surprise." He nodded slightly toward Rafe but didn't take his eyes off Syndelle. Like the night before, she could feel the power radiating off him, cold and ruthless. "What brings you here?"

"I wanted to speak with the girl," Syndelle said.

He cocked his head. "Now what's a soft piece like you want to get involved with one of Big Daddy's girls for?"

Syndelle cast around for an answer that didn't promise more than she could deliver or reveal her curiosity about Skye, finally answering, "I couldn't get what was done to her out of my mind. If I can help you find the person who did it to her, then I'd like to."

Big Daddy studied her for a long moment before saying, "Doc's got her doped up, but you can see her. You can see the other girls, too. Won't do you no good, though. None of them saw the motherfucker who messed them up. None of them remembers anything worth knowing, even with Big Daddy's friend Skye talking to them."

Syndelle and Rafe followed him into the house and down the hallway. The doors on either side were open and the girls inside the rooms looked up as they passed. Toward the end of the hallway, Big Daddy stopped at a doorway and motioned for Syndelle and Rafe to go ahead of him. They entered and moved to stand next to the bed.

The girl was heavily sedated, but even in that state, she was moaning and whimpering, her body flinching underneath the sheet as the horror of what had happened to her followed her into the drug-induced darkness.

From the doorway, Big Daddy snapped his fingers and Syndelle heard footsteps along the hallway—first retreating, then returning to stop next to him, bringing the smell of perfumed flesh and beer with them.

Syndelle studied the girl, wondering again why this human's pain had called out to her. "I don't even know her name."

Big Daddy grunted. "Calls herself Wren."

Syndelle placed her hand on the girl's bare shoulder, allowing her senses to reach for an answer.

For a long moment the girl remained trapped by the drugs coursing through her body, but then her eyes jerked open in alarm, her gaze collided with Syndelle's, and though it was not usually Syndelle's way to take what wasn't offered freely, she let the girl fall into the endless, hypnotic blue of her vampire heritage so that there was no wall separating her mind from the girl's, her will from the girl's.

Because a link had already been formed between the two of them, in the span of a heartbeat Syndelle took some of Wren's memories inside herself and felt the burn of the witch's mark on the girl's hip, as if it were her own. Then pushing beyond that, opening herself even wider, Syndelle moved through the faint traces of violence that still clung to the girl, gathering the psychic particles left by her attacker.

She shivered at the feel of him. At the anger, the need to revenge himself in an attempt to recover what had been stripped from him long ago. The helplessness that burned into a rage so deep and fierce that it would always express itself like this—finding power and release in raping, breaking, and finally carving his message onto the stomach of his victims.

The horror of it washed through Syndelle, aligning itself with the girl's memories of being bound, her head encased in a burlap bag, as her attacker spent hours silently venting his anger. His fear warring with his hatred so that he didn't dare let his victim see his face, so that he didn't dare take the final step and kill his remembered tormenter outright.

For a long moment Syndelle remained trapped in the world of the damned, and then slowly her shields drifted into place, separating her reality from this horror-filled one. She blinked, freeing the girl, freeing herself—for the first time becoming aware of the tears coursing down her cheeks.

Wren slipped away immediately, escaping back into a drugged darkness. Syndelle edged the sheet lower, exposing the girl's beaten, broken body, stopping only when she reached the mark on the girl's hip.

It was a brand, a coven mark, burned into the flesh and intersected by a pair of linked, tattooed pentacles—one of them inverted, symbolizing the second degree of initiation for a witch, the need to face the darkness within and not, as many of the untrained believed, the mark of one who practiced black magic. Syndelle pulled the sheet up, covering Wren's naked body before turning to Big Daddy.

"Are the other girls here?"

He snapped his fingers twice and two girls immediately stepped into the room as though he'd anticipated her request.

The girls had the same look about them as the girl on the bed—young with stringy brown hair and green eyes—though it was impossible to tell if the rest of their features had been similar. One girl had healed, if the misshapen, uneven face could be called that. The other girl's face was still swollen, distorted.

They kept their gazes downcast, only raising their eyes when Big Daddy snapped his fingers, though his attention didn't shift from Syndelle. "You need them to strip?"

Syndelle opened her senses, careful not to trap either of them in her eyes as she tested to see if a natural connection existed between them as it had with the girl on the bed. When she didn't find a link, she focused on one of them and said, "Do you have a brand or a tattoo?"

The girl pulled her sleeves back, revealing bracelets of tattooed barbed-wire, before pulling her shirt up, exposing her breasts and a ring of pentagrams in black and red around one nipple — the lower designs inverted by the artist in order to keep the chain continuous. "I've also got a unicorn on my ass and a butterfly on my ankle. You want to see those, too?" the girl said.

"No." Syndelle's gaze drifted to the girl whose face was still bloated with painful swelling. The girl turned and pulled up her shirt, revealing a back covered with savage swirls, a tangled jungle of surrealist, psychedelic images, including a creature holding a crystal ball containing an inverted pentagram.

Big Daddy shifted in the doorway and the girl moved, not dropping her shirt until she'd shown him her back as well. He nodded to himself before once again meeting Syndelle's eyes. "That all you want with them?"

"Yes."

The girls left without being told. Big Daddy straightened, taking a long swallow of beer before saying, "Big Daddy's got too many girls now to take a personal interest in all of them, otherwise Big Daddy would have seen what the Lady Syndelle saw. Motherfucker must have seen my girls stripping or paid for a private show."

"At Bangers?" Syndelle asked.

He took another swallow of beer. "Could be. Could be other places. Big Daddy's got a lot of action going down around town. So much action that he don't always know which girls are working where unless he's got a special gig lined up for them.

Big Daddy's going to have to ask his boys where these three have been working."

"You'll get word to me when you find out?"

His smile flashed white against his dark face. "Big Daddy'll get word to the Lady Syndelle. Big Daddy'll also let his people know that the lady's got favors coming."

Syndelle nodded, retreating from the room, from the house—surprised and grateful when Rafael enfolded her in his arms as they reached the car, stroking her back and whispering, "Are you okay?" His grip tightening when he added, "I saw what you saw. I felt what you felt."

She hugged him back, taking comfort in his warmth, basking in his concern, her heart tightening with love at the knowledge that he'd slipped into her mind of his own free will, had joined with her as a true mate would when she'd needed him most. "I'm okay."

"Still want to go to Fangs?"

"Yes."

Chapter Seven

Syndelle stared in amazement at the people waiting to get in to Fangs. Her brothers had told her stories about places like this, people like this, but those stories hadn't fully prepared her for the sight that met her eyes.

Like a long black snake, the patrons formed a line, the head positioned at a closed door while the body extended through the parking lot, curling around at the furthest space and weaving back toward the beginning. Body jewelry flashed and more than one of the humans had filed their canine teeth into sharp points. Amazing.

While she'd lived with and been guarded by her family, there was no possibility of visiting nightclubs catering to vampires and those who flocked to them. Even now, if this place weren't co-owned by one with a blood-tie to Brann, she wouldn't venture into it.

"Ready?" Rafael asked. "The sun is going to set in a few minutes. It won't take Brann very long to get here."

"Ready," Syndelle answered before climbing out of the car. Her pulse jumped with excitement at the prospect of meeting Skye, of exploring this new world, even though her heart tripped with trepidation, with anxious foreboding.

She could feel Brann stirring and knew that Rafael was right. The vampire would soon join them.

Last night the nearness of the sunrise had kept Brann from taking her, from closing the Angelini bond by spilling his seed as she held him locked deep inside her. But there would be no reprieve tonight, and once the Angelini bond was closed, he would begin his campaign to make her his companion—he would use the craving of her body for its mates in order to get her to willingly yield everything she was, to grant him power over her by formally accepting his offer of companionship as his blood flowed into her, claiming every cell as belonging to him.

Syndelle shivered, tempted now to keep moving, to race the night and stay ahead of Brann. To run until the sun rose again.

Rafael didn't know what to think as he studied Syndelle. Compared to him, compared to Brann, she was so innocent. So fucking open. She didn't seem to care that he knew what thoughts were going through her head, what she was feeling.

He hadn't expected that. He was used to Brann's thoughts invading his, but only some of them, and only when Brann wanted him to know them.

Shit. Nothing was ever easy. *Nothing had ever been easy* — but at least there'd been a time when he felt like he was in control.

A mocking smile settled on his lips. Oh yeah, right, he'd been in control, big time.

How do you want it? In the ass? In the cunt? In the mouth?

If life was a matter of either getting fucked or fucking someone else, then he might as well get paid for it. Oh yeah, everything had been just great until he'd wandered into that vamp bar down in Los Angeles and got caught up in the scene, raking in the bucks — stripping, playing some other games — all the while knowing that things weren't exactly what they seemed, but figuring he'd handle it.

Right.

But at least he was alive.

He was handling it okay.

Fuck. *Tell yourself another one.*

And now this. Just looking at Syndelle made him want to protect her, made him want to keep her safe from all the pain that he knew was out there. It even made him want Brann to take her, too, so he wouldn't be the only one responsible for her.

Fuck. He'd spent his entire life trying to keep himself safe. He didn't have any practice looking after someone else.

What was he supposed to do with her? An Angelini hunter without the soul of a killer. A female with enough power to challenge Brann.

Rafael couldn't tell how much or exactly why her magic was different, but he could feel something more ancient than the vampire swirling inside her. He didn't need Brann's voice whispering in his head to know that she couldn't be allowed to fall into another's hands—especially now that there was a blood link between all three of them. She might want to run, but this was as far as he was willing to take her.

Sighing, Rafael moved around the car and took her hand in his. And for a moment he was overwhelmed by her emotions, by the wash of pleasure and comfort she took in his gesture. Fuck, she got to him, shooting straight to his heart and moving through the thick armor as though it wasn't even there.

"Come on, babe, this joint is ours for the taking," he said, enjoying the way her nose wrinkled at his gangster imitation.

Syndelle let him guide her toward the door, trying not to stare even though the emotions radiating off the humans danced along her nerve endings and crowded against her senses.

The wolf stirred, rising out of the shadows to view this strange new world through Syndelle's eyes. She smiled as the wolf cocked its head, its expression both perplexed and amused, its thoughts matching hers. *In this the vampires have surely outdone us. To have prey meekly arrive at the dinner table instead of having to hunt it down — amazing — but then again, sometimes the chase is more satisfying than the prey itself. Perhaps these city vampires have forgotten the old ways, the old thrills.*

Rafe laughed, a warm, surprised sound that had Syndelle's eyes rushing to meet his as she realized what he'd just seen and heard.

He stopped and leaned down, rubbing her nose with his as though greeting the wolf. "How real does that get?"

This time it was Syndelle who laughed, heat rushing over her face as she saw his nightmare images of having her shift during sex. "Not that real."

"Good." He pressed a quick kiss to her lips and straightened.

A cheer went up as the door to the club opened and a man stepped outside. *Vampire*, Syndelle thought, and without conscious effort her shields slipped into place as his attention focused immediately on them.

There was no tension in Rafe's body and his voice held only his usual mockery as he said, "So Brann's calling out the big dogs? He send you to escort us inside personally, Gian?"

Syndelle studied the vampire as intently as he was studying her. *So this was one of her…one of Skye's mates.*

He was physically beautiful, with Italian features and hair as black and long as her own, though his was held back by a strip of leather. A ruby stud glinted in one earlobe and his eyes held the midnight sky with no stars or moon, but deep in their centers, a cold, blue flame flickered, drawing the unwary in.

Even without Rafe telling her, Syndelle knew that this vampire was Brann's creation. Her blood hummed with the knowledge like a truth that couldn't wait to be told. She could know his thoughts if she wished, could know his history if she desired. The blood link with Brann and her own magic made it possible, though she chose not to reveal the fact, or trespass into his mind.

"Will you welcome us into your club?" Syndelle asked, a formal courtesy between vampires and the Angelini, between the hunters and their usual prey.

Gian nodded slightly and stepped aside, clearing the way for them. "After you."

Two additional men had stepped outside while Syndelle and Gian studied each other. One was human, bound to the vampires, but not as a companion or a slave. The other was vampire, muscular and blond-haired, ancient in feel but not of Brann's line, or Sabin's.

As she watched, the human checked IDs, allowing those closest to the door to enter, while the vampire moved down the line, picking and choosing, allowing some to go immediately to the front.

Syndelle laughed softly, noticing that those he chose were all blonde women, well-endowed and long-legged. Beside her, Rafe chuckled and squeezed her hand. "Yeah, Roman doesn't believe in a variety pack."

Roman. The name whispered in her blood along with feelings of amused affection. Not Brann's memories, but Sabin's.

"Ready?" Rafael asked, distracting her.

She nodded, letting him lead her inside and guide her to the bar. But when he would have kept moving, taking her to a private table, apart from the excitement and energy of the club, she used their link to say, *No. Let's stay here. I want to watch.*

Amusement rippled back to her. *The show gets old.*

Maybe. But I've never seen it before.

He shook his head as he easily lifted her onto a barstool. *What do you want to drink?*

She bit down on her bottom lip. She'd never been one to drink, a precaution against having her nightmares become her reality. But tonight she felt...alive...as though her childhood fears were old clothes that she needed to shed. *What do you usually drink?*

Beer.

She wrinkled her nose. *Not beer. Name another good drink.*

His smile was mischievous as he brushed his lips against hers. *How about a Slow Screw Up Against the Wall?*

Her heart jumped in her chest, flooding with warmth at his teasing and acceptance. This was what she'd hoped for in a mate.

Fuck. He should have gotten out of her head when the wolf shocked the shit out of him. This was like landing in quicksand, where anything he did was going to suck him down, trap him. She was wrapping him in dreams and emotions that he'd never wanted, never been brave enough to have.

His cock was throbbing, hyperaware of Syndelle's scent, her body heat—aware, too, of Brann moving closer. *Shit.* He should never have teased her about a slow screw up against the wall, because now he couldn't get his mind off what it had been like when she locked him deep in her body. He couldn't stop his body from shivering as he remembered the sight of her sucking Brann's cock as he rammed his own into her tight, nearly virgin channel.

Brann would fuck her tonight as Rafael watched, as he felt her wet mouth around his own cock. Rafael's hand tightened in a fist. He fought the need to grab himself, to try and calm the pulsing, agonizing desire that raged through his penis. He moved away abruptly, heading for Roman's table with its collection of blonde Barbie dolls.

Syndelle watched him go, reluctantly raising the shield between them in order to give them both privacy in their thoughts. The bartender appeared and asked her what she wanted to drink, but she just shook her head, feeling less adventurous now that she was alone.

A human with fanged teeth and silver driven through his eyebrows stopped in front of her, grabbing her arm as though he was going to pull her off the stool and onto the dance floor. But before he could say anything, Gian was there, the flames roaring to life in his eyes. "You don't want to bother this woman," he said, his voice laced with deadly warning and firm compulsion. Dazed, the human turned away.

"I could have handled him," Syndelle said and was surprised by Gian's quick, amused smile.

"If you're like Skye, then you could have." *But I prefer not to waste our patron's blood by spilling it on the floors. And then there is the matter of Brann. Why he has chosen to let Rafael run wild, I don't know. But my sire's will is my will at the present, and he does not want to see you with any man other than Rafael or himself—or one like me, already claimed by an Angelini mate.*

Gian's attention shifted to focus on Rafael, and in that moment Syndelle could feel Brann's presence as though he were standing next to her, looking out of Gian's eyes. She shivered at the display of Brann's power, trying to keep the old nightmares at bay. Nightmares where the wild magic returned. Where vampires who had gained from her blood were hunted by the Angelini in battles that cost the lives of her brothers and parents.

Syndelle braced herself for pain, afraid that she'd find Rafe trying to build a wall between them by accepting the attention of other females. But when she followed the direction of Gian's gaze, her heart lurched—not with pain—but at the sheer beauty of Rafael. Even surrounded by blonde Barbies and sharing a table with Roman, he shone—a perfect blend of masculine strength and feline sensuousness. She could see why Brann had wanted him as a companion. Even without the warlock magic that hovered unclaimed around Rafael, she could guess why the vampire had given Rafe so much freedom.

Whatever events had forced Brann to make Rafe his companion in order to save Rafael's life, it didn't change the fact that the vampire had wanted him, wanted him enough to bind him in the most sacred bond a vampire can share with another. And then Brann had waited—was still waiting—for his companion to offer freely what it was the vampire's right to take.

The knowledge eased Syndelle, making her less fearful should Brann succeed in making her his companion. Reluctantly she turned her attention away from Rafael, glad that for the moment Roman's throng of women was so enthralled by the vampire that they weren't trying to seduce Rafael.

Do not worry, small princess, I enjoy this life after death too much to risk your father's anger or Brann's wrath. I will keep my blonde sheep occupied so that they don't tempt fate by trying to lure your mate into playing with them.

Startled at hearing Roman's thoughts along the link she shared with Sabin, at hearing her father's nickname for her, Syndelle's gaze met the ancient vampire's. Across the distance he winked and she asked, *Did Sabin send you here?*

Of course. Search your memories and you will know who I am, what I am, and how to summon me should you need my help. A grin appeared. *But call only if it's absolutely necessary. As you can see, I have my flock to tend — and Brann is not one I would choose to make an enemy of unless the need was dire.*

Warmth flooded through her, not that she would call on Roman's help, but because her family had found a way to give her comfort without violating the laws of the Angelini prohibiting interference in the binding of one's mates.

Syndelle turned back toward Gian and asked, "Will your mate be here tonight?"

The vampire cupped her cheek and forced her eyes to his. He made no attempt to mesmerize her, but seemed content to study her intently. "You have the same eyes as Skye." He gave a slight smile. "And my sire assures me that he knows much about the Coronado family, and that she is one of them, though he did not see fit to share this information with me until now. I have called her to me and she will be here shortly."

Excitement raced through Syndelle, making it hard to stay still. She hadn't really doubted that Skye was her missing sister, but having Brann confirm it — and like a flame roaring to life, the chiming in her mind became a dark call, warning her that the vampire had arrived.

Gian dropped his hand from her cheek and she turned to watch as Brann moved into the nightclub. Power and lethal menace radiated off him, and like gazelle in the presence of a tiger, the humans moved out of his way, parting even on the dance floor so that his path to Syndelle was clear and direct.

She laughed, lighthearted with the realization that here, in this moment, she did not fear him. In this place, with her excitement over Skye and the knowledge that Roman stood guard, she could relax and get to know her mate before they returned to the house and finished what they'd started the night before.

Brann cast only a quick glance in Rafe's direction, frowning when he saw Roman, but then his eyes were locked on Syndelle's. "Dance with me?" he purred, and her body tightened as though a rough tongue had glided between her legs and over her nipples.

With a thought, she knew that he'd directed the disc jockey to play a slow, sultry song meant for lovers. The wolf rose, its body flushed and ready, but because Syndelle had already accepted that she would complete the mating, the wolf hung back, the chiming of the Angelini magic fading, allowing her time, postponing the moment when they would overwhelm her.

Syndelle moved into Brann's arms and was immediately surrounded by his warmth, his power, his scent. They enfolded her like a protective blanket, making her feel safe and cared for.

Her heart rate spiked in response as a shaft of fear pierced through her contentment. *He was an ancient being. A master of illusion and compulsion.*

As if sensing the direction of her thoughts, he held her more tightly against his body and said, "We will be bound together for all eternity, Syndelle, and I will care for you and keep you safe. You are mine, a precious gift I never thought to actually possess."

Syndelle shivered, knowing how thoroughly he planned to possess her. But she could feel no attempt to get through her shields, and slowly, as he stroked her back, she relaxed and accepted his caring. He would keep her safe—from everyone but himself—and yet, she was not defenseless. She might not be a hunter like the rest of the Angelini, but she wasn't without her own power and magic.

The first song moved into a second slow song and she smiled against Brann's shoulder, wondering how long Gian would allow him to control the music.

Brann pushed her hair aside and lowered his mouth to her neck, sending a bolt of fire through her bloodstream as he pressed kisses along her exposed skin.

I have not fed since I rose. Do you offer what I need, Syndelle? Or should I feed from one of the humans drawn here for that purpose?

Her heart stuttered in her chest but she whispered in his mind, *Take what you need.*

Joy rushed through Brann. He had not planned on asking this of her so soon, but the moment her body was pressed against his, the need had risen, hungry and overpowering.

His lips moved to the base of her throat and he paused only long enough to ensure that the curtain of their hair provided privacy before letting his fangs drop and sink into her tender flesh.

She jerked against him, a sharp blending of pain and pleasure, and he could feel the Angelini magic coursing through her blood and spilling into his body, making her an addiction, a need he would always crave. But if that was the price he had to pay to possess her, he was willing to pay it.

He drank, sating one hunger while another roared through his cock and in his tight, swollen balls. There were back rooms here for the vampires to use, but he would not take her in one of them. This night was too important and theirs would be no hasty coupling, but a beginning that would last until the sun rose, and beyond.

Reluctantly he withdrew his fangs, washing over the puncture marks with his tongue, taking pleasure in how her body was soft and the scent of her arousal filled his nostrils. He would grant her time to meet Skye, but then they would return to his home and finish what was started last night.

With ease, his mind reached Gian's. *Does your companion answer your call? Or does she still amuse herself by proving that she can defy you?*

And you have done so well with Rafael? But in answer to your question, Skye is pulling into the parking lot as we speak.

Good. Though I am curious, I would allow Syndelle privacy as she visits with her sister for the first time.

Show her to my office, then. I will bring Skye.

Chapter Eight

❧

Come, Brann said, leading Syndelle from the dance floor as the slow song ended and a fast one took its place. *Your sister will be here in a moment and Gian has graciously volunteered his office in order to afford you privacy.*

Syndelle frowned, remembering Gian's comment about not knowing Skye's origins. "You knew she belonged to the Coronados. Yet you did not send her to us," she said as Brann ushered her into the office, anger smothering her earlier contentment with her soon-to-be mate.

Brann's eyebrows lifted. "Your family has made it known that an Angelini daughter was missing?"

Syndelle's anger softened to confusion. Brann stroked her cheek. "There have been whispers over the years that Sabin's daughter was taken, but none knew the details, and most thought it more likely that some accident had befallen her and your parents' grief prevented them from speaking openly about their loss. When I saw Gian's mate for the first time, I knew otherwise. She is your father all over again, in looks and disposition." He shrugged and a soft smile played over his features. "But there has been little time to attend to the matter. And now you have come along…"

Brann leaned over, pressing his lips against the spot where his fangs had pierced her flesh. *I can grant you some time alone with her because I know it is important to you, but we need to finish what we started, Syndelle. We need to close the bond — for your sake as well as mine and Rafael's. I would prefer to do so without racing the sun.*

Thank you, she whispered in his mind, unable to stop herself from wrapping her arms around his waist and taking comfort when he pulled her into a hug.

Skye Delano studied the blond vampire and his collection of women and frowned. "I haven't seen him here before."

Gian laughed. "He has been in the area for a while, but usually seeks a higher class of prey."

"So why is Rafael with him?" The frown on Skye's face deepened as a new blonde strolled over to the table, leaning down so that her breasts threatened to escape the tight, thin top and press against Rafe's face. "Why isn't he with Brann and this woman that your sire says is my sister?"

Gian shrugged. "Brann is a power to himself. I gave up trying to understand his motives long ago." His look was speculative as he studied Rafael. *Though perhaps Rafael has been the lure and that is why Brann has allowed him free rein to fuck as many women as he wanted.*

A surprising rage slid through Skye, leaving her feeling uncertain and confused. She did not like the idea of this unknown woman being trapped by Brann, and yet she had no reason to feel anything toward her except curiosity.

Gian smiled slightly and leaned in to press a kiss to her forehead. *I can feel your emotions. Relax. Even for one such as you, it is normal to be anxious and uncertain about this meeting and what it will reveal about who and what you are.*

She nodded, acknowledging his comment. For so many years she'd had only vague, emotional memories of her life before she'd been found in a ghetto of Los Angeles, a silent child with no history, no name. There'd been hazy thoughts of a happy time spent with a mother and two fathers, followed by the wrenching agony of separation, and superimposed over all of it, the driving need to survive.

She'd even gone so far as to have a computer hacker retrieve her records from the social services department. But there was nothing that she didn't already remember.

She'd been trapped in silence until she'd discovered the ability to hypnotize and sink into a self-induced state of being *other*. Until then, any attempt at speech had caused a sharp skull-piercing pain to rip through her mind. Any attempt at remembering her origins had also been met with excruciating agony.

Only later, after she discovered the reality of vampires, had the veil between her memory and conscious knowledge partially lifted. In her mind's eye, she could now see the face of her mother's vampire mate, a face like her own — her blood father — and she could now remember being trapped in his gaze as he commanded her to silence, to forget her origins if she was ever lost to them.

Even now, it sickened her to think of all that she'd endured because of his command. She'd been too young to understand what he meant by silence, and so the compulsion had lodged in her mind in its broadest context — causing her to suffer needlessly. And now the past had arrived in the form of a sister.

They paused at the door and Gian knocked as a courtesy before saying, "Brann and I will return to the bar while you speak with Syndelle. You have nothing to fear from her, and perhaps nothing in common, but I think you will like her in the same way you like your human mate's family."

Brann pulled away just as a knock sounded and the office door swung open. For a moment Syndelle's heart stilled as she took in the woman who moved into the room with predatory grace and all the confidence of an Angelini hunter.

She is your father all over again, in looks and disposition, Brann had said, and he hadn't lied.

The door closed, leaving the two women to study each other cautiously, like wolves meeting for the first time.

The blood hummed through Syndelle's veins in recognition of their kinship. Skye's eyes narrowed, as if she too felt the connection but wasn't sure what it meant. Finally Syndelle broke the silence, saying, "Do you remember anything about the Coronados?"

Her sister's face tightened almost into a snarl. "Only bits and pieces of it. Sabin, the vampire. Riesen, the werewolf. Pictures of them, along with a woman. I don't even know her name."

"Richelle Coronado." Syndelle hesitated, not wanting to insult Skye, but unsure of how much she knew of their ways. "Among us, the children are always given the last name of the Angelini. The Coronado line goes back to the very beginning." She paused again, finding this meeting more difficult than she imagined—seeing in Skye the same thing she saw in their brothers and in their parents. The confidence. The sureness in themselves.

Syndelle was not surprised that Skye didn't remember much of their parents. It was ancient custom to try and protect Angelini children by making them forget their origins so that they would blend in among humans should they go missing for any length of time. After the loss of their daughter, and after enduring the agony of not knowing what had happened to her, their parents had broken with tradition and added the extra safety measure of reinforcing the blood-link with Sabin so that he could call their children home or touch their minds in order to find them.

Curious, Syndelle asked, "How did you come to be called Skye?"

"I picked it, then I refused to answer to anything else." She shrugged. "Eventually the social workers decided I must have finally remembered my name, so they changed the paperwork to agree."

"Our parents called you Jovina. It means 'daughter of the sky'."

Jovina. The name resonated in Skye, touching a deep chord and vibrating through her. "How was I separated from them?"

"You were taken from their compound by a young female from Riesen's pack. She was there with four others, watching you while our parents were away. When they got home, they found the others drugged and you missing. But by the time they tracked the female, she'd been killed and there was no sign of you."

"I ended up in Los Angeles."

"They found the body of Riesen's pack member in New York."

Skye sighed, frustrated and saddened by the loss of her memories. It had never bothered her before—at least not in the same way. But it was different now that she had mates—especially a human mate with a large extended family—a family that loved fiercely, and still treated her with wary courtesy.

As if sensing the direction of her thoughts, Syndelle moved closer, taking Skye's hand in hers. The low humming in Skye's blood turning into a roar between one heartbeat and the next.

"Blood to blood," Syndelle said. "I can give you my memories of our parents and our brothers." Her smile twisted somewhat ruefully. "Though you will see them through my eyes, and me through theirs. How they react to you when you know them will be much different than how they react to me. You are like all of them, while I am like none of them."

Skye studied the dark-haired woman in front of her. *Soft. Almost human.* Those had been her first disappointed thoughts when she saw Syndelle. But now Skye saw something else. There was a quiet strength in her sister. A quiet courage. A patient, ancient quality that spoke of old magic.

Before taking mates and learning that supernatural beings existed—and that she was one of them—Skye had lived her life alone, relying on herself, trusting no one completely other than herself.

And now this woman stood in front of her, offering a priceless gift—but to receive it would require Skye to trust her. And surprisingly enough, she realized that she did. "I'd like to know them, through your memories until I form my own."

Syndelle's smile was a mixture of relief and pleasure and mirth. "I'm told you always carry at least one knife. I'll need it to make a small cut on your palm."

Skye pulled her hand from Syndelle's and reached for the switchblade in her back pocket, opening it before handing it to her sister. Syndelle set the knife down on one of Gian's office chairs and said, "I need your left hand."

When Skye gave it to her, Syndelle began tracing something on her palm and Skye's heart jerked in reaction. She could almost see the strange, unfamiliar symbols that Syndelle was drawing.

Gian's presence stirred in her mind and she allowed him to see what she was seeing. His alarmed puzzlement moved through her as he said, *She protects the two of you from harm using wards that she is not old enough to have mastered.* His attention shifted to the knife on his chair and his voice went to a demand. *What do you plan?*

I'll tell you later, Skye said, closing the link and grimacing when his displeasure, if not his exact thoughts, washed down their link.

"Keep your hand here," Syndelle said, releasing it to write a ward in the air before moving to trace symbols on her own palm. When she was finished, she reached for the knife and with a steady, smooth movement sliced across Skye's palm and then her own before joining their hands so that the blood of one met the blood of the other.

Almost instantly Skye plunged into a dark abyss, terrifying in its very emptiness. She struggled instinctively to escape, knowing that her heart was thundering in her chest, though its beats were absorbed in a silence so complete that nothing could ever penetrate it, a silence so deep that it was everything and nothing, a beginning and an ending. Rage threatened to claim her, a reaction to the terror that would take its place and make her helpless if she allowed it. But before she began to fight in earnest, the void changed, becoming more like a dark wineglass being filled with deep, rich, ancient blood—and suddenly Skye was drunk with memories. Syndelle's at first, and then Sabin's, moving through the time before Syndelle existed and going backward until the moment of Skye's birth.

A blink and Skye found herself standing in front of her sister, crying—overwhelmed by memory and emotion—by her parents' pain at losing her, the joy of knowing their love—for the past that had been lost and found, for the future. She didn't resist when Syndelle hugged her, holding her until she could gather her control.

When Skye finally pulled out of the embrace, she could feel Gian at the edges of her mind, frantically demanding entry, she could hear him pounding on the door as though he couldn't enter his own office.

He can't, Syndelle said, surprising Skye with the sound of her unspoken voice. Instantly Skye searched for the mental link and found that she couldn't block her sister's access to her thoughts nor could she touch her sister's mind at will. But before panic or anger could set in, Syndelle said, "Look deeper and you will find the connection we share through Sabin's blood. This new, other pathway between us already begins to fade, just as the wound on our palms does. In a few minutes your thoughts won't be even a whisper in my mind." She wrinkled her nose and gave Skye a mischievous smile. "Though in truth, I can hardly hear anything beyond the yelling of your mate and the demands of my own future mate."

I'm okay! Stop banging on the door! Skye sent to Gian and felt his instant relief. This time she didn't close the link between them. "You were able to lock him out of his own office?" Skye asked, returning to her earlier thoughts, seeing again the quiet strength in her sister, the quiet courage, and the patient, ancient quality of old, old magic.

"I will release the wards in a second and then I must leave. But before I do, I wanted to speak with you about Big Daddy's girls. I'd like to help you search for their attacker."

Denial sprang instantly to Skye's mind, but almost immediately she recognized its source in the memories that weren't her own. She had no reason to turn away Syndelle's help—other than the fact that Brann's displeasure at the idea flowed to her through Gian in a cold wave. A smile widened her lips. "I'd like your help. It'll give us some time together."

"I'll find you tomorrow, then." Syndelle paused before adding, "I visited Big Daddy's house today. What I learned is with you now, though I did not draw your attention to it earlier."

Her words jolted Skye. She hadn't felt her sister's presence at all.

Syndelle's hand raised, her fingers moving again, this time tracing symbols in the air, dropping to her side a second before the office door flew open and Gian stormed in, followed by Brann.

Skye picked up the knife, her movement slowing her mate and diverting his attention. She grinned at his vampire reaction to the presence of an Angelini with a sharp blade and he scowled, coming to a halt next to her and reaching for a tissue on his desk, handing it to her so she could clean the knife before putting it away.

Brann tilted Syndelle's face, forcing her to stare into his eyes and Skye felt a stab of fear that wasn't wholly hers. Gian's hand went to her wrist halting her as she took an unconscious step forward. *Do not interfere. It is against our laws and the laws of the Angelini.*

Skye tensed, not caring about rules she knew nothing about, but then Brann gently brushed his thumb across Syndelle's lip, and she saw her sister's soft smile. Skye's alarm at seeing Brann with Syndelle lessened somewhat, but didn't completely fade even as she accepted that this wasn't her fight.

Wise decision, Gian said, his voice laced with sardonic amusement.

Brann released Syndelle and she moved to Skye, giving her a hug, touching Skye with her thoughts again. *You know the way home now. Look deep inside yourself and you will find it hidden behind safeguards that only you can pass through. Our parents and brothers are away from the compound. But it doesn't matter. Before they return, they will come here to reclaim you. You will never be lost to us again.*

Anticipation and excitement rippled through Skye, along with a heady mix of other, much less-familiar emotions. She hugged her sister back. "I'll see you tomorrow."

The wolf rose then, restless, and Syndelle reluctantly slipped from her sister's grasp, knowing that it was time to move into another, more carnal embrace. The wolf had been patient, granting her time, adding its strength of will to her own as she'd guided Skye through the ancient, powerful magic of blood memories, but now the wolf was hungry for its mate.

Syndelle placed her hand in Brann's and allowed him to lead her from the office, down the short private hallway and out into the loud, throbbing, human-filled club. She looked and found Rafael still at Roman's table. The wolf looked, too, and didn't like seeing him surrounded by other females.

A low growl rumbled through Syndelle's mind. A sound she'd rarely heard. With it came a command to go over and stake her claim, to make it known that she would rip the skin from any who tried to take her mate. The hair rose along Syndelle's spine as the wolf's hackles rose and its body stiffened, prepared to fight, prepared to stalk over and herd its wayward mate home, then show him that he didn't need to look elsewhere for his pleasure.

Next to her, Brann laughed, and Syndelle knew that he was in agreement with the wolf. But when he would have sent the command for Rafael to join them, Syndelle stilled him with a squeeze of her hand and a plea. *Allow me my pride, too, Brann. I don't want to have to force him to my bed any more than you wish to force him to yours.*

Surprise rippled through Brann, and pleasure. Surprise that she had touched so accurately on why he hadn't yet claimed Rafael completely, though he had lusted after him from the moment he'd first seen him. Pleasure that she seemed at ease with his desire for another man.

As you wish, he told her. To Rafe he said, *The choice is yours whether you join us or not.*

The wolf stalked around in Syndelle's consciousness, growling, unhappy about leaving one of its mates behind.

Perhaps he will join us, Syndelle told it, her own heart heavy that the Boxster was not behind them as they pulled into Brann's driveway.

The wolf snarled, almost making Syndelle dizzy as it continued its restless pacing.

In an effort to calm the spirit inside her, Syndelle shifted so she could view Brann's profile. *And what of this mate? You were anxious to claim him earlier. Is he not good enough by himself? Have you decided that he is unworthy of your attention?*

Immediately the wolf stopped pacing and sat down, cocking its head and breathing deeply of Brann's scent before its eyes dropped to half-mast and its tongue moved over its lips. Syndelle laughed, a sound that drew Brann's eyes to hers as he stopped the car.

"You're at peace now with leaving Rafael behind?" His voice was a purr that had both Syndelle and the wolf shivering.

"Yes," Syndelle said, waiting for him to go around and open her door, to draw her out of the car. Another laugh escaped when he swung her into his arms and carried her into his house, not setting her down again until they reached his bedroom.

Though she hadn't seen it before, it looked exactly how she would have envisioned it. A huge, elaborately carved antique bed stood in the center, surrounded by a room full of richly colored tapestries and priceless artifacts—all guarded by strong wards and charms.

His hands went to her tank top and she obediently raised her arms so he could slip it off her. The bra was peeled away next, followed by the rest of her clothing and her shoes. For a long moment he did nothing, said nothing, as his eyes roamed over her body, and then he took his own clothing off and stood, allowing her to look at him.

There hadn't been time to truly appreciate his body before, but now Syndelle became lost in the sight. He was like a heavily muscled big cat, a tiger, predatory grace married to incredible strength.

She couldn't stop herself from stroking him, from exploring his shoulders, his chest, the hard male nipples.

His cock jutted between them, fully aroused, leaking, huge and thick with heavy balls hanging beneath it. When her hands stalled at his chest, he growled, his hips moving slightly as though demanding that her explorations continue downward, and a small thrill of feminine victory tightened Syndelle's body.

An unfamiliar tenderness assailed Brann. He'd thought to claim her the moment he had her back in his home, but somehow she'd once again turned the tables on him. She was a surprise that he found himself enjoying. A treasure he could savor in so many different ways.

Even her escape from his compound hadn't truly angered him. Nor had her show of independence when she so easily kept both him and Gian from knowing what transpired with Skye.

And now that he could mount her, riding her body until she locked him to her and closed the bond, he found himself willing to wait, willing to let her take the lead in this mating dance—at least for a little while.

His hands speared through her hair, tilting her face upward for his kiss. She moved in and the feel of her soft, hot skin against his almost undid his intention to allow her time. His tongue thrust into her mouth, stroking in and out like his cock would soon do in her channel. She whimpered and pressed against him, trapping his penis between them, unconsciously rubbing against it, making the fire in his blood roar hungrily. When he pulled his lips from hers, satisfaction joined the raging need. Her mouth was swollen, her breathing fast, her eyes filled with desire—the honest desire of a woman for a man—not the magic-induced mating lust of the Angelini or the thrall of vampire fascination.

He eased her onto the bed, settling himself on her, kissing and stroking her, praising her with his thoughts as her hands explored his body, rubbing and petting, making him shake with need as he had not done in centuries—not since he was a human male. When she guided him to her entrance he thought his heart would burst with happiness, with excitement, with anticipation—with the sheer need to couple.

And then he was inside her, held in a warm fist of female flesh as she whimpered softly underneath him, her hands raking across his buttocks and driving him deeper, compelling him to thrust, to savor, to claim. She cried out, kissing his chest, nuzzling his tight nipple and a different hunger roared to the surface.

His fingernail extended, sharp and deadly, a weapon—but this time he turned it on himself—opening a gash so that blood flowed over his nipple. And then it was Brann who was crying out, desperately thrusting as she took his blood, her pulls on his nipple as he fucked her more erotic than anything he'd ever experienced—either as a man or a vampire.

He pounded in and out of her, fighting off the need to orgasm for as long as he could, but finally the demands of his cock, the tight ache of his balls, couldn't be ignored any longer.

He pressed his need to come onto her, sharing with her the exquisite ache that rode him, that was almost painful in its intensity, and she cried out, accepting his will, clamping down on him, her release causing his penis to jerk inside her, spewing his seed in a hot blast of pleasure.

It was like opening the gates and allowing a wild, howling, magic-filled wind to rush in.

He felt the change in her immediately, the demands of her Angelini heritage, and he rolled to his back, taking her with him, her body still joined to his, his blood answering the call of hers, his heart thundering in his chest as her mouth went to his neck, biting down so hard that she broke the skin, sending fire racing through his bloodstream, a scorching wave of exquisite agony that had him growling, only barely able to keep from rising and putting her on her hands and knees.

Her lips and tongue tortured him as she licked and kissed her way down to the spot over his heart before marking him. Then she levered herself off his body and returned to the place on his inner thigh where she'd claimed him the night before.

Nothing in his existence had prepared him for the mating lust of the Angelini. His blood roared, rushing through his mind and heart and cock in an incessant chant to claim her, to mount her and drive himself deep into her channel, to pound into her until there was no barrier between them, until they were one body.

There was no fighting it.

When she lifted her head from his groin he pounced. A giant predator intent on only one thing, taking its mate.

He bit her, marking her in the same way that she'd marked him, and then she went willingly to her hands and knees, her legs spread, displaying the swollen, glistening folds of her labia, her channel dripping with arousal and the seed he'd spent earlier. The sight of it inflamed him, and he covered her body with his, driving hard and deep in a single thrust as his fangs sank onto the spot where her delicate neck met an equally feminine shoulder.

Wild lust raged through him, a primordial call that sprang from the oldest magic, from the very forces that had created all life, mortal and supernatural, prey and predator. It commanded his body as if he had no will of his own and he had no defenses against it, could do nothing other than ram his penis into her, desperately plunging in and out until finally a deep hidden place inside her opened, trapping the head of his cock, milking him of his seed repeatedly, claiming him completely and making him an Angelini mate.

* * * * *

Rafael dragged in at sunrise, his cock hard, his heart twisting painfully in his chest, a ball of confused emotions rolling in his gut. He'd stayed away, but it had cost him.

He found Syndelle in Brann's bedroom, asleep in Brann's bed. The one room, the one place in the house that he'd never dared to enter, until now.

Rafael moved to the side of the bed and undressed, studying Syndelle as she slept. She looked like an angel. One that might bring him salvation. Or damnation.

He couldn't bear the thought of climbing into his own bed and sleeping alone now that she was here. And so he did something he'd fought since the night Brann was forced into making him his companion—he slipped into the vampire's bed, knowing that after the sun set, they would all three be in it together, knowing that he was one step closer to becoming Brann's lover.

Rafael closed his eyes against images of being taken by Brann while Syndelle watched, of being taken while he devoured her pussy with his mouth, while she writhed underneath him as his cock filled her at the same time Brann tunneled in and out of his ass.

Unable to stop himself, Rafael wrapped his hand around his shaft, pumping, squeezing, knowing that a man's touch was so much different than a woman's, but no less pleasurable.

His buttocks clenched and he groaned, arching into his own hand and rousing Syndelle with his thrusting. She moved over him, covering him with her body, opening herself, offering him a safe place, and Rafael cried out, accepting the sweet haven that she freely gave, the bond between them wide open—the shining willingness of her heart to love him almost more than he could bear.

They hadn't forced their pleasure on him last night, but he hadn't been able to keep from opening the link between them and knowing what they were doing, what they were feeling. And now he needed the touch of Syndelle's body against his, not just for sexual release, but for comfort.

He let her ride him, his hands rubbing over her breasts, her back, wanting to cry out at the intimacy of having her above him, her dark curtain of hair falling on either side of his face, trapping them in a world of their own.

She leaned down, brushing his lips with hers, licking lightly at the seam of his mouth, a gentle offering, a wolf greeting its mate, and he groaned, pulling her down and rolling with her so that he was on top. "Oh god, Syndelle," he whispered, his thrusts becoming rough, desperate, as he took her mouth with his, as her hands stroked his buttocks before her fingers trailed along the crevice between them, brushing over the pucker of his anus and sending him careening out of control.

Chapter Nine

୧୨

Syndelle studied Rico, Skye's human mate, before turning her attention to the other policeman with him. Detective Augustino. She didn't need the wolf's recognition to know that Detective Augustino was more than just human. The cock of his head when she'd walked in with Rafe, the flare of his nostrils, followed by a swift flash in his eyes when her scent had told him that she was mated to both a human and a vampire, were enough for her to know that he was a werewolf.

It surprised Syndelle to find him here. Pack members usually lived close together and worked in businesses owned by the pack.

Unless they were outcasts. Or loners. Or had been sired by one on a human female—and had not yet joined a pack.

For a moment, uneasiness rolled through Syndelle, but the wolf urged her to take Augustino's scent, to taste his flavor. When she did, she found nothing that hinted of fear or hatred, and so she relaxed.

Rafael lounged in a casual sprawl on the couch, next to Syndelle, his leg against hers, his touch comforting.

Skye joined them, sitting on Syndelle's other side and looking at Rico, her knee brushing against his and causing him to shift in his chair as his eyes went dark with arousal and the front of his pants stretched tight over an erection. Syndelle smiled, pleased for her sister, pleased at the obvious desire between Skye and her mate. Rafael snickered and Skye broke the eye contact with Rico, her attention shifting as she dropped a folder on the coffee table. "Here they are."

Augustino leaned forward in his chair, placing a folder next to Skye's. "When Rico did a run for attacks on female strippers with a particular tattoo, it hit my desk. Over the last year there have been four unsolved homicides here, all with the same victim profile—male, blond with long hair, inverted pentacle tattoo somewhere on the body." He frowned. "The first two of them had a goat's head drawn in the center of the pentagram. The second two didn't. There's a fifth victim. No tattoo on him, but the damage done to him was identical to the other four, so I think he was killed by the same perp. All five victims were roughed up, shock burns consistent with a cattle prod, sodomized—ass and mouth—with genitals removed as a final insult. Amazingly enough, the powers that be have managed to keep a lid on it. Probably because three of the men were strippers, one was a male prostitute, and the other was a drifter. Up until last month, another cop was working this case. Now I'm here and it's mine." His gaze brushed over Syndelle and Rafe to settle on Skye. "And if we catch this guy, then we play by human rules. Understood?"

Skye scowled at her mate, but agreed. Augustino gave Syndelle a piercing look and she nodded. He tapped the folder and said, "These aren't for the faint of heart," pausing for a moment before opening the folder and spreading the pictures out like cards in a horror deck.

Syndelle's heart lurched, not just for what had been done to the victims, but at how closely the men resembled Rafael. With a curse, Rafe stood and moved away, the rush of his emotion almost overwhelming Syndelle. She brushed her mind against his, silently offering to comfort him, but not pushing her presence on him.

He surprised her, opening his thoughts to her rather than closing himself off. Showing her his memories of one of the men whose photograph now lay on the table. Justin. He'd been a stripper in Los Angeles, at a club named Tinker's, just as Rafe had once been before his life had intersected with Brann's.

She felt Rafael brace himself for her reaction. *It doesn't matter*, she whispered in his mind before additional memories followed, of Rafe selling his body—just as Justin had done, of the two of them laughing about the men who used them, even though they were both crying—both dying a little more inside.

Unable to stop herself, she rose from the couch and joined Rafael by the window. *It doesn't matter*, she repeated, stroking along his spine, directing his mind to what it had been like earlier, when he'd joined her in Brann's bed—to the pleasure they'd shared, a pleasure given and received equally. He hugged her to him, accepting her comfort before giving her a kiss and leading her back to the sofa.

"You okay?" Rico's voice sounded gruff, uncomfortable, his hand toying with Skye's where it rested on his thigh.

Rafael nodded and touched one of the pictures. "I knew this guy. He was street-smart."

Augustino shrugged. "Not smart enough. Or not careful enough."

Syndelle stiffened, the wolf rising from the shadows, both of them ready to attack the detective for his insensitivity to their mate's pain. Only Rafael's rush of surprised gratitude held Syndelle to the couch long enough for his voice to whisper in a gentle caress. *I'm okay. It's okay. It was a shock seeing Justin's picture, a reminder of things I don't like to remember.*

Some of Rafe's old amusement returned. *But if it's all the same to you, I'd rather not have to tell Brann that you're in jail and he can't fuck you or feed from you when he rises tonight. You may have avoided becoming his companion so far, but that doesn't mean he would take your absence with good grace. He's not always...pleasant...when he has to wait.*

Syndelle heard his words and accepted them, but the wolf couldn't refrain from locking its gaze to Augustino's. Its stare making him sit up straighter while something dangerous moved through his eyes a second before he nodded his head slightly in acknowledgement of the wolf's warning that to mistake its mate for a weak human of no consequence would be an unpleasant, possibly fatal mistake.

The tension eased and Skye freed her hand from Rico's and leaned forward, opening the file she'd placed on the table. Syndelle recognized Big Daddy's three girls, but not the other two.

Skye separated the photographs of Big Daddy's girls from the others and told Augustino what she knew of them, before moving to the girls Syndelle didn't know and saying, "These two are independent workers as far as I can tell. Rico got a hit on them last night." Skye touched one of the photographs. "So far she's the only one I've been able to find out anything about. Goes by the name Yvonne on the streets. She used to hang out at Bangers, but no one can remember her stripping there. Had a job as a waitress at some burger joint near the strip, and sometimes turned tricks on the side. She may have left town or she may be holed up in Vegas. I haven't found her yet. The other one I'll start looking for today."

Augustino leaned forward and tapped the picture of the fifth girl. "Save yourself the trouble. She's dead. Pulled her out of a crack house a couple of weeks ago after they got a shooter in there. Hit by a stray bullet. I was close to the location when the call came in." He shifted his attention to include all the pictures. "Got dates to match the attacks?"

Skye flipped the photos over and lined them up according to when they'd been attacked. Augustino consulted his notes, adding dates to the backs of his five photographs and lining them up.

Rico grunted. "Boy, girl, boy, girl, all the way down the line. But the boys end up dead, though he doesn't carve anything into them and he doesn't try to destroy their faces. Still possible there are two perps here. The MOs are different enough." He leaned forward, shifting through the papers in Augustino's folder. "No pattern where he picks up the men, other than he's got to be seeing them somewhere he can get a look at the tattoo. Strippers are pretty obvious. The male prostitute and the drifter both had the tattoos on their chests. Could have seen them without their shirts. Could have seen the four of them without hiring them first for a quick fuck." He looked at Rafe, then Augustino. "The last guy he killed, Justin, he the one without the tattoo?" When Augustino nodded, Rico continued, "The girls are trickier. Tattoos wouldn't have been obvious on all of them. So maybe with them he goes for a certain look, gets a better one as a paying customer, then abducts them later. That would also explain why he puts a bag over their head."

Syndelle closed her eyes, recapturing the feel of the man behind the attacks, but it was Rafael who spoke for her, also remembering what he'd felt through their link. "This guy hates the women more, but he's also more frightened of them. That's why he covers their faces, so they won't see him. He's not brave enough to kill them yet, but he wants to."

"Then it's only a matter of time before he gets brave enough," Augustino said.

Syndelle opened her eyes and studied the faces of the victims. The girls all looked very similar—almost as though they were the same girl. But over time, the faces of the men had changed somewhat, as though it mattered less and less to the killer that the man he was killing be an exact match to the one in his memories. "This is the only way he can get his power back. Even when he's finally killed the female who tormented him in the past, he won't stop. And perhaps eventually the tattoos won't be what determines which woman he chooses as his next victim. He'll seek only to empower himself."

"Fuck," Rico growled.

"He'll choose a male victim next," Skye said, stiffening when both Rico and Augustino turned their attention to Rafael.

"No," Syndelle said, her heart screaming with fear as she read their thoughts on their faces.

"Yes," Rafael countered, closing his mind to her and expecting that she would honor the thin barrier. Instinctively she reached for Brann and found him alert, his thoughts and will uncharacteristically absent, though she could sense there was no barrier between *him* and Rafael.

"This guy does kill the men, Rafael," Skye pointed out, her tone a blend of concern and mocking humor.

Rafael shrugged, sprawling once again on the couch.

Syndelle's frown deepened and the wolf stirred restlessly. Neither of them liked the idea of Rafael being in danger. Or the thought of him exposing his body to others.

Return to the compound then. There is no need to involve yourself in this human business, Brann said and immediately Syndelle felt shamed that she'd let her resolve falter, that she'd thought only of keeping her mate safe, that she'd momentarily forgotten what she'd seen and felt when she'd touched Wren's memories. Her hand moved to Rafael's and as if sensing her need for contact and reassurance, he entwined his fingers with hers.

Augustino leaned forward, studying his notes. "I think it'll be enough if you get a tattoo, just in case that's still a trigger for the guy we're looking for, and then we'll have you troll several different clubs. We don't have time to put you in one place and wait for the perp to stumble across you."

Rafe's lips quirked upward. "Not a real tattoo. I'm not into body art."

"And not the Sigil of Baphomet," Syndelle said. "Only the pentacle."

"The Sigil is the tattoo with the goat's head?" Rico asked.

Syndelle nodded, reaching for both Brann and Rafael, finding in them the same resolve with respect to the Satanist's mark.

Augustino shrugged. "Sure. No problem. At this point, I don't think it makes any difference to the perp as long as it's inverted. I'll ask some of the guys in vice what they use. They're in and out of tattoos all the time."

Syndelle felt Rafe's dismay at the prospect of going to the police station and it lightened her heart somewhat. *You volunteered for this*, she reminded him.

He brushed his fingertips over the back of her hand, seeing beyond her words. *It'll be okay. Trust me. Compared to some of the things and situations I've encountered since becoming Brann's companion, this is easy. And it's not as though I'm in it alone.*

Syndelle nodded slightly. Skye said, "Any feel for when this guy is out looking for his male victims? Big Daddy's girls work days and nights. Same with Yvonne. So our guy could have seen them anytime."

"Anytime," Rico said, "but not just anyplace. It looks like he prefers trolling along the edge—rough places, but not so dangerous that just getting out of the car is life-threatening." He shot a look at Augustino. "You got these plotted on a map?"

"Yeah." Augustino pulled out a map and spread it across the table. "Don't get your hopes up. First thing we looked for was a pentagram pattern. Blue dots are where the victims worked or were known to hang out. Red is for the body dump."

"You mind if I pencil in where the women were taken and found?" Skye asked.

"Help yourself. Use a letter. A for abduct. B for body. I'll color-code it when I get back to the station."

Skye checked her notes and marked the map. When she leaned back, they all saw it. "A circle," Rico said, "or close enough. Probably doesn't even know he's doing it. And it still covers a lot of territory."

"Maybe not," Skye said. "He's got to find places where skin's going to show. I say he approaches the men directly, solicits them, or offers drugs so they'll go with him willingly. He's not worried about showing his face. He already knows he's going to kill them. That'll knock out some of the rougher bars where the men would kill him if they thought he was coming on to them."

Rico nodded. "Any gay bars in the circle?"

"One." Skye's mouth widened into a smile. "The Hole."

"Oh, Christ," Augustino muttered. "Couldn't they have come up with something better than that?"

Rico snickered. "Case is all yours, Augustino. Enjoy yourself."

"What about other clubs?" Syndelle asked.

"Bangers, Stingers, Quaduum, Nuggets. Those are the ones I can come up with off the top of my head," Skye said. "And they're all places our victims have been, or would have fit in at."

"Let's work from there," Augustino said. "It's as good a place as any to start with."

They spent a little while longer discussing strategy and timing, then Rico and Augustino left. "So are you hanging with Syndelle and me 'til show time?" Skye asked when Rafael made no move to get off the couch.

"Give me a remote control and point me to the TV room and I'll be happy to let you two visit without me—as long as you don't leave the house. Brann'll have my ass if Syndelle goes anywhere unguarded."

Skye smirked. "Like Brann doesn't already have your ass."

Chapter Ten

Rafe threw back his head and laughed before saying, "Curious, Skye? Somehow I don't think you'll ever see that show with your human mate. But maybe if you're lucky, Gian will take you to one of the clubs where vampires gather to feed and fuck their companions and slaves. Of course, to enjoy the entertainment, you've got to be part of the entertainment." Now it was his turn to smirk. "But maybe that won't be such a stretch for you." Rafael brushed his fingers across a scar on his neck. "The last time Brann was around when Gian was taking care of you, I paid the price."

Skye's eyes narrowed and opened, doubt warring with curiosity as she remembered Gian saying, *You are my companion. Among our kind, the sharing of blood with a chosen one is often done in front of close friends*, as she *also* remembered how he'd brought her to orgasm with his hands twice while in the company of other vampires. She turned to Syndelle. "Is he jerking me around?"

"He doesn't lie. I have heard of such places, though the Angelini do not frequent them."

Rafael snorted. "Only because they have their own places, and the Angelini who are bound to Weres like to attend the Howls with their wolfie mates." His grin widened. "Now those are supposed to be real fuck-fests. Not that I've ever been to one. Thank god. Running through the woods while a pack of wolves chase me for pre-coitus entertainment doesn't sound like fun to me."

Once again Skye's gaze sought Syndelle's. Syndelle nodded slightly. "Chasing a condemned human is not done often, though it is not against the laws we have all agreed upon—if the human's crime is grievous enough to warrant such a death."

Syndelle smiled teasingly at Rafael. "Though my human mate is delicious and would temp any Were, he would not be welcome at a Howl. Rarely are humans allowed at a pack's gathering. The Howls are held to encourage breeding and mating among the purebreds—so that more females will be born—though sometimes an Angelini female who has not yet found mates is sent in the hopes that she will bind two wolf packs together by mating with the alpha from each of them." A private, satisfied rush of heat warmed Syndelle. She'd thought perhaps she would find at least one mate among the Weres at the Howl she was supposed to attend in the company of Riesen's pack, and her parents had perhaps hoped she would find two, but both she and the wolf were well satisfied with Rafael and Brann.

"What about the other?" Skye asked. "Do the Angelini have fuck parties?"

Syndelle's cheeks warmed and she tried not to think of their parents involved in such activity, but she did not turn away from the truth. "Yes. Privately. Among Angelini who are close to one another. And there is rarely a sharing of one's mates."

Skye looked at Rafael. "Are there clubs in Vegas where vampires and their companions and slaves go to fuck and feed—as you so delicately put it?"

"Yeah. Why? Interested in going to one?" Rafe shifted his position and grasped Syndelle's hand, pulling her onto his lap, then wrapping his arms around her and hugging her tightly against him, his body vibrating with suppressed tension despite his external show of amusement.

"No, thanks," Skye said, moving to sit on the chair opposite them. "So are slaves willing or are they made against their will?"

"They are supposed to be willing," Syndelle said, shivering at the thought of being a vampire's slave. "But few understand the irrevocable contract they agree to when they take a vampire's blood, exchanging their souls and their will for whatever it is they hope to gain from their new master. Some call themselves servants rather than slaves, but in truth, they are chattel, to be used and discarded as a vampire sees fit."

"Discarded as in killed?"

"A vampire has the right, though it is frowned upon, and rarely is it necessary. Deprived of the blood of the master, a slave often commits suicide. But it is more common for a vampire to simply give the servant to another to use as he or she wills."

Skye frowned. "There are humans at Fangs who have a blood-tie to Gian, but he swears that they aren't servants, that he protects them by giving them his blood."

"Your mate speaks the truth," Syndelle said.

The doorbell sounded and Skye rose, opening the door for a whirlwind of a female whose first words were, "Oh god, I've made a complete ass of myself," before she noticed Syndelle and Rafe and added, "Again. Shit. Sorry. I didn't know you had company."

"My sister Syndelle and her boyfriend, Rafael." To them, Skye said, "This is Rico's cousin, Francesca."

Syndelle rose, smiling at the flustered girl, before saying to Skye, "We'll go home for a while and meet with you when it's time to go to The Hole."

Skye's smile was grateful. "Thanks. See you later. If we have time to try and track down Yvonne, I'll give you a call."

Rafael and Syndelle returned home, moving almost automatically to his bedroom, stripping without words being necessary, as the need for physical contact became as essential as the need to breathe.

They tumbled to the bed, but when Rafe would have covered Syndelle's body with his and fucked her, she resisted, pushing him to his back, playfully holding his wrists against the comforter while she leaned down to toy with the barbell piercing his nipple, sucking and biting and pulling it with her teeth.

His cock jumped in response, a pant escaping as his back arched, pressing the nipple deeper into her mouth. She shifted position so that she could admire the defined muscles of his chest, the washboard abdomen and his engorged penis as she lowered her upper body and offered him her own nipple. Her cunt lips swelling, her clit standing at rigid attention, waiting for its turn to feel Rafe's lips and tongue.

Rafe groaned, latching onto Syndelle's offering like a starving man, laving and biting roughly, grasping her nipple with his teeth and pulling on it like a greedy puppy at its mother's teat. Fire streaked through Syndelle's belly and she reveled in her mate, wanting to wallow in his scent, his desire, in the sounds of pleasure he was making.

He shifted to her other breast, and she kissed her way over to his other nipple, playing with it, sucking it until his pleas and his hands urged her lower.

She went willingly, dragging her stomach over his mouth, mimicking the dart of his tongue into her belly button with a lick and twirl into his navel, before traveling the last short distance to heaven and pressing her swollen clit into his mouth as she licked over the head of his penis.

Lust roared through Rafael, as hot and demanding as the female flesh above him. He wrapped his arms around Syndelle's hips, hugging her wet cunt to his face and burying himself in it. He was starving for her, desperate for her, completely addicted to her. He wanted to spend all day licking and sucking, making her cry and beg and shiver and writhe, but already his balls were tight, his cock tortured as her mouth and hands worked him, bringing him to the edge of release again and again, only to deny him.

They were both shaking, panting, almost to the point of no return when he rolled, ripping himself away from her so that he could watch her face as he took her, as his cock shoved into her cunt, as she cried out, wrapping her legs around him, welcoming and holding him tight in honest passion and blossoming love.

His lips sought hers, his tongue mimicking what his cock was doing. He pumped in and out of her, the pressure and anticipation building with each hard, deep stroke, until finally he was locked in the heaven of her body, his semen rushing through his penis in wave after wave of sweet agony.

Afterward they lay cuddled together, his cock still deep in her channel as they absorbed each other's heat and essence. Idly Syndelle traced his spine, smiling into his shoulder at the way his buttocks tensed when her fingers drew near them.

"How did you end up with Brann?" she asked, bracing herself against his withdrawal, letting him know with the touch of her mind to his that she would accept his refusal if he chose not to answer.

He stilled and she could feel his internal struggle, until finally Rafe exhaled, a heavy sigh that seemed to deflate him. He pulled his head back so that he could meet her eyes, giving her a smile so fragile she feared that any movement on her part would chase it away.

I'll show you if you want to see it, he said, the offer touching her so intimately that her heart felt like it was going to burst.

She nodded and Rafael lowered his head, brushing his lips softly against hers. *I've never had anyone like you in my life. It scares the shit out of me. If you care about someone, it only makes it worse when they discard you like you're trash.*

"Are you really afraid of that happening, Rafael?" she whispered. "You're no slave, you're a companion and a mate." *Do you really think that anything you could show me would make me turn from you?*

I don't know.

Then show me the worst and find out.

The very worst was locked away in his childhood. A guilt that even he couldn't face most days. What he could show her made him laugh and shake his head. "The worst is sexual and you don't seem to shock easily."

"Sex is hardly a new discovery—for humans or supernatural beings. There is little that doesn't get talked about among so many brothers, and my parents have not shied away from explaining things." Her face grew somber as she added, *Everything in my life has been centered around protecting me and teaching me to guard myself in the hopes that once I found my mates and claimed them, I would be safe.*

Rafael could sense there were deeper meanings and fears behind her words, just as there was overlaying sadness and uncertainty about whether or not she would be loved for herself and not just because the Angelini magic made it impossible for her mates to refuse her. He couldn't stop himself from reacting, from giving a tender, self-conscious laugh. "We're a couple of fucked-up vampire companions, aren't we? Brann probably wonders what he did to deserve us."

His small joke brought tears to Syndelle's eyes and warmth to her heart. "Speak for yourself, I'm a mate, not a companion."

"Yet," Rafe whispered, covering her mouth with his, teasing her lips apart and stroking inside, conveying with the gentle brush of his tongue against hers that he wasn't driven only by the animal instinct to mate, that her love and acceptance were becoming essential to him.

For a long while they lingered, exploring each other, enjoying each other, their bodies moving in unhurried rhythm as they swallowed each other's soft cries of pleasure. When they were finally sated, it was Rafael who said, "Do you still want to know how I became his companion?"

"Yes."

"Watch then," he said, pulling up the memory for her to see.

Chapter Eleven

"Easy money," Frankie, one of the strippers standing with Rafe, said as he changed into his street clothes. "And they're all loaded. Fuck man, how many times do you get invited to a private club like Drac's?" He rolled his eyes. "Fucking Goth with class. Better than this wannabe place we're working now. And who knows, maybe you'll hook up with someone, play the slave to their master." Frankie's smile turned sly. "Maybe that guy who's been sniffing around you for the last couple of weeks will be there."

"Brann?" another male stripper asked. "I'd fuck him in a heartbeat. You're crazy for giving him the brush-off, Rafe. He's got the only two things that matter. A big dick and money. Bend over and spread your cheeks for him and you've got it made."

Rafael shivered and his cock stirred thinking about Brann. Fuck, what was wrong with him? In the old days he'd have just gone with it. He knew Brann wanted him. And god, he couldn't even be around Brann without getting a hard-on.

His stomach tightened. Maybe it was just working at this place. At first the wildness had appealed to him, but lately—shit, he'd wake up covered with sweat and think about not showing up for work.

Rafe buttoned his shirt and threw his working clothes into a gym bag. At least he didn't remember the fucking nightmares. That was something. Then again, he'd had a lifetime to perfect forgetting. Maybe it was time to swing the other way for a while. Not that the outcome was any different. Male or female, he was just a pretty toy, a vacation fuck or an arm-piece until something better came along. But hell, it paid the rent. And it wasn't like he threw his money away on dope. A few more years of working and he could own his own club if he wanted to. There were days when the idea appealed to him—not here, though, not in LA. He was getting tired of the plastic people and the fake glitter, all of it hiding an ugly soul-stealing underbelly.

"You coming?" Frankie asked, his eyes looking a little wild, like maybe he'd gotten a bad mix of whatever he was using.

A cold finger traced Rafe's spine and he shivered, afraid for a split second. He shook it off. Fuck that. He was done with being afraid. "Sure, I'll come."

"Oh yeah, he'll be coming all right," one of the other strippers said.

"Hey, okay if I go with you guys?" another stripper asked.

Frankie shook his head. "No. Only got an invite for Rafe this time."

Rafael's heart rate spiked and he cut a look over at Frankie, suspicion and misgiving squaring off with a gut-curling sense of anticipation. Yeah, he and Frankie knew each other, but they weren't friends. So why the invite? Why not take one of the others instead? Unless maybe the invite had really come from Brann.

Fuck. He should hook up with Brann and get it over with. Play the game. Enjoy the ride. Try not to get attached. Try not to forget that despite what any of his lovers told him, nobody was going to take him home to meet their parents. Used goods. Damaged goods. Fucked-up goods. It was always the same in the end. He'd go with Frankie tonight, see what happened, and then he'd stay away from the scene for a while. Maybe work some of the clubs catering to rich women wanting a fantasy fuck while their overweight doctor husbands swallowed Viagra and fucked their golf buddies' wives.

Rafe followed Frankie out to his car and got in. Yeah, if Brann was behind the invite, he'd spend some time with him. And after they were done, he'd swing the other way for a while. He liked women and men pretty much equally, though with guys it was easier. They weren't looking for an illusion of romance to justify raw, sweaty sex.

Drac's. He'd never been in it, but from the outside it oozed class. The front parking lot was a wet dream of exotic sports cars and old classics. Anyone not driving one was relegated to the back, not that anyone was allowed to park their own car.

Fuck, the guy who'd taken Frankie's piece of shit car acted like he was going to have to go home and change his uniform after sitting in it. And Frankie, what the hell was his deal?

Rafe knew Frankie was a user, meth and ecstasy a lot of the time, but he'd also take whatever hot new party drug was making the rounds, but fuck — the closer they got to Drac's, the more amped Frankie got. Like a junkie who was just about to score big.

They got to the front door of the club and a cold breeze moved along Rafe's spine before reaching into his gut and circling it with ice-cold fingers. What was wrong with him tonight? He half-turned, thinking he'd blow this off and call a cab to come get him. But then he saw Brann's red Viper pull in. Fuck. What was it about Brann that had his cock standing at attention just seeing him?

Rafe shook his head and turned away, his lips curling into a mocking smile. As many times as he'd been fucked — literally and figuratively — you'd think he would have learned. Hope was for fools and cold cash would take you further away from your past than any illusion of love — no matter how fucking hot your partner was.

He started to follow Frankie into Drac's but the doorman stepped in front of him, blocking his way, intoning in a voice and accent that matched the butler outfit like they'd come right out of a prop shop catering to Hollywood, "Do you enter Drac's of your own free will?"

Rafe watched as Frankie disappeared down the hallway, an invisible man the doorman couldn't see or couldn't be bothered with. Or maybe Frankie was a regular here—of the party favor persuasion—so the hired help didn't need to play their roles with him.

"Yeah," Rafe answered and the butler-outfitted doorman stepped aside.

Fuck. Club wasn't exactly the right word for Drac's. It was a theme-roomed orgy-fest.

First room on the right. Women only. Some on the floor doing it to each other while others sat on couches like they were at a tea party, watching, being eaten out by women kneeling in front of them.

First room on the left. Whips and chains and all the kind of things Rafe avoided like the plague. He would *never* willingly allow himself to be helpless. Never again—not that he'd ever *allowed* it in the first place.

Next rooms, more of the same, though with mixed sexes and a lot of biting and sucking and even some blood thrown in. Shit. It got old. Like there weren't plenty of terrifying things in the world without people pretending to believe in vampires.

He ended up in a larger room. Crowded. More like a club scene with dancing, drinks, body-rubbing and come-ons, some leading to a trip to the front rooms, some leading through doors guarded by bouncers.

The casually dressed mingled with the elegantly dressed while waiters and waitresses wandered around in skimpy costumes, sporting slave bands around their necks and wrists and ankles, batting their eyelashes and smiling in a way that said they were here to serve more than drinks. Rafe pulled a beer off a fancy serving tray and surveyed the room, looking for Frankie, but not seeing him—and not really caring. He didn't need to hold Frankie's hand. Hell, he didn't need to hold anyone's hand. One scene was pretty much the same as another and he knew his way around all of them.

His penis stirred and his buttocks tightened, anticipation washing over Rafe a second before Brann's cologne did. "What are you doing here?" Brann asked, the purr in his voice like a heated fist around Rafe's cock. *Fuck, how did he do that?*

Rafe shrugged. "Thought I'd check it out."

"Leave now. You don't belong here."

Rafe's smile curled in mocking self-defense. "Fuck off."

Brann's hand closed around Rafe's arm and sent a shaft of heat straight to his dick as Brann pulled Rafe around to face him. "Leave now," he repeated, something in his voice making Rafe want to listen and obey. Rafe shook it off. Shit. At Bloody Mary's, Brann had seemed laid-back—no, those words would never describe him—less threatening, that'd do it.

But not now. Not here.

Here he was all predatory grace. Domination in a way that would strip a lover to his soul.

Shit no. Rafael couldn't handle that. It'd be like bathing in acid and when the bath was done there'd be nothing left but a mass of scars. "Fuck off, Brann. You don't like the scenery, change rooms. There's enough action here for everyone."

Brann stiffened, dropping his hand and shrugging, as though he was sorry he'd bothered with Rafael. He moved away then without another word.

Rafe's gut roiled. He was tempted to leave, but no way was he going to do that now. Still, he turned, not wanting to watch Brann hitting on someone else.

The woman behind him smiled. Blonde beauty in a barely there outfit. Deadly sex wrapped up in a beautiful package and Rafe decided he was willing to open it. He smiled back. Practiced charm that promised he knew how to please a woman in the bedroom.

She moved over to Rafe, brushing against him, licking her lips like he was a feast she couldn't wait to sink her teeth into. "Fight with your boyfriend?"

"Hardly. He's just some prick who didn't like seeing me here." Rafe smiled. Yeah, fuck Brann. He could take care of himself. He knew how to work a scene. "Tried to send me home like a bad boy."

She licked her lips again, toying with the expensive pendant around her neck. "Umm, and are you a bad boy?"

"I can be, if that's what you like."

Pale fingers moved down the center of his chest and trailed over his aroused cock. "Ishana likes bad boys," she purred and he wanted to roll his eyes and say, Fuck, not another wannabe actress talking about herself in the third person, so full of herself that she hadn't bothered to notice that the erection didn't have anything to do with her. Not that she wasn't capable of giving him one, but he was standing at attention because she'd moved over before Brann had disappeared from sight. She pouted, a pucker of lips that Rafe could easily imagine sucking him off. "Come upstairs with Ishana," she said.

His cock jerked. Yeah, he'd come upstairs—in her mouth, in her cunt. There were probably rubbers next to the bed, but he had some in his back pocket anyway. He wasn't stupid enough to go anywhere unprotected.

He let her lead him to a bouncer-guarded door and once again had to answer the question about his willingness before it was opened and they climbed an elegant set of stairs. When they got to the top, surprise diverted some of the blood from his cock. Couples, singles, and groups of people mingled around antique furniture, drinking from crystal glasses as they talked and laughed, a Renaissance drawing room except for the way its inhabitants were dressed.

A few of them looked up, tittering when they saw Ishana. "Ignore them," she said. "They're just jealous."

Right. Rafe's eyes went back to the scene even as Ishana continued to lead him toward an open doorway along the side of the larger room. Like downstairs, some of the people in this room were acting out their vampire fantasies, sucking at their partner's necks, or chests, or in one case an inner thigh.

It was strangely erotic in this setting, and Rafe's cock responded, despite the fact that he had no desire to play it out himself. He shifted his attention, finally noticing that this room was ringed with doors leading into smaller, private rooms. Most were closed, but a few were open, the sounds of sex escaping like background music.

Ishana stopped in the doorway to a bedroom, giving Rafe a flirting, teasing smile. "Do you enter freely?"

Fuck. Couldn't they think of something more original? Answering the question another time was two tired times too many. It was almost enough to kill a hard-on. "Yeah."

She stepped back and let him enter first. When she didn't bother to close the door behind her, Rafe started to say something, then shrugged it off. If she wanted to scream and moan so her buddies in the other room would hear her getting fucked, it was no skin off his dick.

He stripped then reached over and pulled her clothing off. She stroked the pendant and licked her lips. "Fuck me first, then we can move to the real fun."

Rafe shrugged. Fine, he could do that, though the air moved over his skin and raised the hair on his arms. He put on a condom before tumbling them to the bed, willing to take the bottom or the top but she rolled, angling expertly so that his cock shoved into her pussy before she'd even finished wrapping her legs around him and pulling his face down to hers for a kiss.

He managed five strokes before the sting of leather whipped across his shoulders and back. "What the fuck!" He levered himself up and off the bed, cock still rigid, condom glistening with her cunt juices.

The woman wielding the crop was coldly beautiful, pale blonde like Ishana but with fire-and-ice eyes, and a pair of fangs that would have made Rafe laugh if his shoulder didn't sting and he wasn't so pissed off. His attention shifted for a second to the woman on the bed and disgust roiled through his gut at the way she was staring avidly at the other woman, masturbating as she watched the true object of her desire in action.

Fuck. Not that he cared if two women were hot for each other. Hell, he'd worked two at once on more than one occasion and helped them work each other, but he didn't go in for the whipping shit and he sure as hell didn't like being set up. They could play with someone else if this was what turned them on.

He jerked the condom off and threw it in a trash can, then bent to retrieve his clothes. The crop blistered his shoulders with heat again and he stood. "Don't do it again, bitch."

"You have violated our most sacred law and I claim the right to judge you for your crime." She slapped the crop against her own leg and within seconds two men wearing slave outfits and jewelry appeared at the doorway, moving in and grabbing Rafe's arms, dragging him out to the larger room despite his curses and his attempts to fight his way free.

Don't give in to the fear became his mantra as soon as he realized that some of the people in the room were feeding on his thinly disguised panic, enjoying it more than the fucking kangaroo court taking place in front of him. Rafe relaxed in the grip of the men holding him, settling his lips into a mocking smile, as though it was all beneath him and he was bored by the stupid game.

The doorman was called. The bouncer was called. A man who'd been standing close to the bedroom was called. And every one of them answered the same, "I heard him say that he entered of his own free will."

There was a dramatic pause in the room, a swelling of anticipation in the seconds before something powerful washed over the crowd. And then Brann was at the top of the stairs, his presence, the look on his face, sending relief through Rafe along with a flow of hot blood to his penis.

"You go too far, Lilith," Brann growled, directing his attention to the woman who'd wielded the crop. "Release him."

"He is mine to punish as I please," she said. "He was fucking my companion without permission."

Brann made a dismissive gesture. "Your companion lured him here."

Lilith's smile grew more vicious. "Perhaps. Perhaps not, Brann. Regardless, it isn't your concern. Our rules are quite clear. Any human who willingly enters this club is subject to our laws and our judgment. My companion is clearly marked with my pendant and yet this human fucked her without first gaining my permission." She turned to the members in her "audience" and said, "Do all agree, he is mine to punish, even unto death?"

There was a murmur of agreement and she smiled. "Then death it is and I invite all to join in the feast of his blood."

In that instant, Rafael knew they were playing this game with deadly seriousness. He started struggling again, receiving another blow from Lilith's crop for his efforts.

"Do not strike my companion again," Brann said.

Lilith's face twisted into a sneer. "You have not claimed this pathetic human, Brann, so do not try to keep him from his punishment."

"I have claimed him informally, and now I make my claim known to all. If you choose to kill him, then I will claim the same right and will destroy Ishana for seducing what belonged to me."

"If what you say is true, then my companion is blameless. She didn't know he belonged to you. He claimed no relationship with you."

Brann's smile was condescending. "Your companion took the word of an angry human, one who'd been told to go home and reacted by flaunting his disobedience. I have heard no one say they witnessed her formally asking if he belonged to another and was free to offer himself to her. After all these centuries, one would think Ishana would know better."

Lilith turned, hatred burning in her eyes when she looked at Rafe. "Do you belong to him?"

Rafael didn't hesitate to lie. "Yeah, bitch. I do."

She raised her hand, wanting to strike out, wanting to disfigure and then kill him, but Rafe saw her fear of the consequences as surely as he read the knowledge that this whole event had been staged to lash out at Brann.

"Then claim him, Brann," she said, turning her attention back to her audience. "Claim him in front of all of us so that we know you both speak the truth."

Rafe's eyes met Brann's and he shivered, seeing the hard purpose in them. Seeing once again the predatory grace that had spooked him earlier. The domination of will that would strip a lover to his soul.

Brann moved to stand in front of him. Rafe mocked, "Going to say 'I told you so' now?"

Something flashed in Brann's eyes, amusement perhaps, before he flicked a glance to either side and said, "Release him."

The men dropped their hold on Rafael, but there was nowhere to run and so he didn't attempt it. His gaze met Brann's and he didn't shy away when Brann pulled him close, holding him so that his erection pressed against Brann's, separated only by the other man's clothing.

Brann's eyelids lowered as he touched his lips to Rafe's in a first kiss that only hinted at what was possible between them. Despite the audience, Rafe responded, opening his mouth wider and meeting the thrusts of Brann's tongue with his own. Enjoying the power and strength and easy confidence of Brann's embrace.

Brann tightened his grip, making it impossible for Rafe to break the contact or end the kiss, and then true fear ripped through Rafe as he felt fangs elongate in Brann's mouth. His tongue scraped against them in his hurry to break the kiss, filling both their mouths with the metallic taste of blood.

Vampire! Rafe screamed silently, his heart thundering in his chest as he tried to struggle against Brann. The fight lasted only a moment before he felt lightheaded. Before the metallic taste changed in flavor and Rafael somehow knew that Brann had also nicked his own tongue.

Brann shifted slightly, brushing their cocks together, and Rafe felt only intense need, intense desire, a longing like he'd never known. He couldn't stop himself from sucking on Brann's tongue as though he could draw nourishment from it. *You will belong to me for all eternity. A companion is not a casual bed partner*, Brann said and Rafael couldn't work up any fear at hearing the voice in his mind. *Do you understand?*

When he didn't answer immediately, Brann's tongue retreated and Rafe nearly cried out. *I understand*, he said unable to free his lips and answer with his voice.

Right now my will calms you, but in a moment I must release you and formally ask if you wish to be my companion. If you deny me, then I will not be able to prevent Lilith from punishing you, from draining your blood and offering you to the others like a pig brought for slaughter.

It was a fucking setup!

Yes, and had I known what Lilith intended I would have protected you from her games.

Anger rushed through Rafe and he wanted to strike out. *Why didn't you just take what you wanted? You could have done me at the club and moved on to the next piece of ass that interested you and they probably wouldn't have even bothered with me.*

Perhaps. But what's done is done. Do you think I want to tie myself to an unwilling companion?

Then don't do me any fucking favors. Even as he thought it, fear moved through Rafe, a fear that Brann would answer his challenge and abandon him to the others.

One of Brann's arms tightened around Rafael's waist, while the other dropped, freeing Brann's hand to move around and grasp Rafe's still-rigid penis. *Accept my medallion when I offer it to you. Or die if you wish. The choice is yours. The choice will always be yours, Rafael.*

Brann's hand tightened on Rafe's cock for a moment, sending shards of ice-sharp desire through the shaft and into his balls even as Rafe wanted to scream at him to go to hell.

I know you'll fight me, Rafael, even if you save yourself by becoming my companion. So I'll tell you now, deny my claim to you afterward if you must and for as long as you choose, fuck who you want in rebellion, Rafael. Brann's thumb brushed against the head of Rafe's cock, smearing the pre-cum around before tracing a symbol that Rafe felt all the way to his soul. *But you will not come again unless it's in the arms of one you are bound to by blood and magic.*

Rafael almost cried out when Brann released him, stepping back far enough to unbutton his shirt and remove a short chain with an ancient-looking coin from around his neck. "Do you accept my offer and freely choose to become my companion?" Brann asked.

"Yes."

Rafe's stomach tightened as one of Brann's nails elongated, turning into a deadly claw before touching the spot over his heart and opening a gash. "Then bind your life to mine by taking my blood and wearing the medallion that shows all that you belong to me."

Rafe moved forward, pressing his lips to Brann's flesh, taking what was offered and losing himself in a sensual heat, feeling Brann's possession and will invade every cell in a hot rush, not surfacing again until semen jetted through his cock in an endless wave of ecstasy.

Chapter Twelve

Syndelle welcomed Rafe's semen into her body, holding him to her as he shivered, hugging him as he calmed. He gave a shaky laugh before lifting his face from her neck and saying, "Sure beats the hell out of coming all over the front of Brann's expensive shirt and trousers."

Her eyes widened in amusement at the image his words provoked. She pressed a kiss to Rafael's mouth and ran her fingers down his backbone, teasing him with light strokes at the base of his spine. "It was a small price to pay for something so valuable as your life."

Rafe's eyes met hers and she could feel his desire to believe that he was truly worthy. She kissed him again, a soft offer of reassurance followed by a rub of her nose against his, and when the wolf rose inside her, she let it turn the gesture into a greeting, into a show of satisfaction with its choice of a mate, Syndelle's tongue licking across his lips in the second before the wolf disappeared, making Rafael laugh. "Good thing it takes a lot to freak me out these days."

Skye called a little while later, tempting them from the cocoon of Rafe's bed by saying, "I think I have a lead on where Yvonne is. Want to ride along with me when I go to talk to her?" When they arrived at Skye and Rico's home for a second time, she joined them in front of the house. "Sorry for the interruption earlier."

"Rico's cousin is all right?" Syndelle asked.

"Depends on who you ask." Skye's smile faded somewhat. "Rico's family tends to be..." She shrugged. "Almost every one of them works in law enforcement. Francesca seems flighty and high-spirited to them, which leads to conflict, and she seems to have a penchant for doing and saying things that leave her mortally embarrassed."

Syndelle sensed the underlying sadness in Skye, the desire to be accepted by her human mate's family. She took her sister's hand in hers, the low humming in her blood turning to a roar before Syndelle mentally turned the volume down and with a thought showed Skye how she could do the same. "Give them time. They will come to see the light shining inside you and the love you hold for Rico. They will come to understand how lucky he is to have been chosen by an Angelini, by you."

Skye frowned and Syndelle stilled, accepting her sister's mental probes, allowing her to find the blood connection between them and follow it to Syndelle's thoughts. *This is our family pathway?* Skye finally asked.

Yes, through our mother's blood, through the Coronado line, and through Sabin's line. You will always know when you are in the presence of one who is related to us.

The hum? Skye tried to think back to the Angelini she'd encountered at Big Daddy's.

Yes. Though it will not be so loud with the others as it is between us.

Skye's frown deepened. *They'll be able to read my thoughts at will?*

It is no different than the link between you and Gian. Syndelle's smile held just a hint of mischief. *And I have seen you keep him from your thoughts.*

Skye studied her sister, meeting her gaze, not realizing what she was looking for until she didn't see it. Instead of the cold, eternal flame of the vampire that she saw in Gian's eyes, and that Rico swore he sometimes saw dancing in hers, there was nothing in the centers of Syndelle's pupils except a blackness so vast that it made Skye shiver as she remembered the dark abyss, the terrifying, silent place she'd experienced before Syndelle shared her memories.

In a heartbeat, foreign thoughts pressed on Skye. Commands whose origins she could only guess at. Warning her that even though Syndelle had formed a bond with Brann, she must still be guarded closely. Hinting that in the future there would be those who would do anything to destroy her sister, and still others who would slaughter to possess her.

Skye blinked and found herself staring at very human eyes. Blue eyes so similar to hers that it was like meeting her own gaze in the mirror. Shrugging off the strangeness of the experience, she said, "Ready to go?"

Rafe grinned. "You'll have to drive, unless you want Syndelle in your lap."

Skye frowned at the Boxster. "Not a very convenient car. Don't you and Brann have something less conspicuous and more practical? I can't believe this thing hasn't been stolen and parted out by now."

Rafe laughed. "Only someone with a death wish would be stupid enough to try and steal it."

"Right. And your common, lowlife thief is going to know this car belongs to a vampire because…?"

"I can see you and Gian spend all of your time fucking." Rafe ran his hand over the hood of car. "He obviously hasn't taught you what every good companion needs to know, how to avoid stealing property that belongs to another supernatural."

"Yeah. Stealing cars is something I do every day," Skye said, her mind seeking Syndelle's as curiosity overrode her uneasiness at still knowing so little about the world she found herself a part of.

"Find the place in yourself that you call *other*, Skye. Look at the car through those eyes. See the magic instead of the prey signs you usually hunt," Syndelle said and Skye could feel her sister's willingness to show her, but also her confidence that she could find what she was seeking on her own.

She concentrated, amazement leaving her momentarily stunned. "It's like seeing another world layered over the one I'm used to seeing," Skye said, her voice hushed and awed. Strange symbols screamed from the surface of the Boxster, and while she couldn't read them, the warning they shouted would have battered through the subconscious of even the most drug-crazed car thief.

Her eyes moved to the coin held on a chain around Rafael's neck. For a moment it looked ordinary, appearing as it always did. Gian's voice whispered in her mind, warning her to brace herself in the second before Rafe's hand touched hers and Brann's power rushed into her, a psychic lightning bolt that had the power to kill.

Gian's voice was amused as he repeated a warning he'd given her several times before. *Never forget that Brann is a force to be reckoned with.*

I'm starting to see that.

Good.

Skye turned her attention to her own companion medallion. And like Rafe's, it looked ordinary at first, but as she watched, the ruby at its center darkened in ominous warning, issuing a clear message easily read by a supernatural—that she was a vampire companion to one of Brann's line.

Her eyes met Syndelle's, and it was almost as if something warm and furry rose up inside herself, and with that sensation, the part that she'd always named *other*, took shape, becoming something separate and yet inexorably entwined, the wolf of Riesen's line greeting the sister wolf she saw staring back at her in Syndelle's eyes. And for the first time in her life, Skye felt fully whole. As though she'd finally found all the missing parts of herself. As though she now could offer her mates everything she was.

Gian's caress was almost as real as a physical touch. *Trust me. We have not felt cheated. Now go and deal with this human business you feel compelled to involve yourself in. The sun will set in a few hours and the night does not last long enough for me to share you*—a ripple of lust moved through them both—*except with Rico. He will join us tonight?*

Perhaps. Skye let the wolf and her Angelini senses fade so that the world around her looked as it always looked. "Yvonne's staying at a place not far away from Bangers," she said as she opened the door and slid into the Boxster.

Syndelle settled on Rafe's lap, comfortable despite the tight fit. Glad for the physical contact and warmed from the inside out by the feel of his erection against her buttocks.

As if it ever goes away, he teased and she snuggled closer, suddenly wishing they were alone, that they could couple again. His arms tightened and she could feel the answering need flare through him.

She tilted her head, giving him access to her neck, to the place he and Brann had repeatedly bitten. Rafe pressed his lips to her skin, sucking on the spot, sending heat to her nipples and clit, along with comfort to her heart.

Skye parked the car and got out, laughing as she said, "I'll give you two sixty seconds to decide whether you want to cool off and come with me or stay here and come with each other."

Rafael lifted his head and snickered. "Very funny." He reached for the door and swung it open, giving Syndelle a gentle hug before shifting her to her feet and getting out of the car himself.

"This is a residence hotel?" Syndelle asked, taking in the despair-coated walls, and the sunken, hopeless nature of the people she saw sitting on their small porches, smoking, or drinking, or simply staring into space.

"Residence hotel. Shithole," Rafe said. "Take your pick."

They followed Skye into a dull-gray hallway, holding their breaths as they trod on carpet smelling of urine and vomit. Skye stopped in front of the last door on the right and knocked.

Footsteps sounded on the other side of the door before it was flung open, as though the person on the other side had no concerns about what she might find waiting for her. There was a second of recognition in Yvonne's eyes, of core-deep fear, before she slammed the door shut and refused to respond when Skye knocked again.

"We could probably force it open," Skye said, but felt oddly reluctant to do so.

"No. We can't," Rafe said.

It took a second for Skye to put it together, to join the fact that Yvonne's face bore no evidence of the vicious attack she'd suffered, with the sensation of foreboding she felt at the thought of forcing the door open and pushing her way into Yvonne's room. She found the mark near the base of the door and crouched down to get a better look at it, guessing, *She's a vampire's companion?*

Syndelle joined her, both of them careful not to let their knees touch the fetid carpet. "A slave."

Skye frowned. "She recognized at least one of us and was afraid."

"Yes."

"Why didn't her 'owner' kill our killer?" Skye's frown deepened. *I've assumed he's human. Am I wrong?*

I have found nothing to suggest he is other than human. Most likely she traded her life to a vampire in exchange for being healed.

What's so special about her? Why would a vampire bother? The vampires I've encountered at Fangs view most humans as little more than food and an occasional plaything.

"Did you see the telescope at her window?"

"No," Skye admitted. "Her reaction took me by surprise."

Rafe moved so that his legs were against Syndelle's back, steadying her. "Can you tell who she belongs to?"

Syndelle rubbed her fingers along the symbol carved into the wood, the dark-colored crevices filled with Yvonne's dried blood. "No, the mark pronounces her a slave and binds her to the room, protecting her from harm while she's in it, but whoever made her a slave left no trace of themselves."

Rafe helped them both to their feet. "Let's see what she's watching through the telescope."

Skye grimaced. "I don't know about you two, but I'm suddenly being hit with wave after wave of compulsion to get out of here."

Rafe laughed, a flash of white teeth and challenge. "And you'll obey, of course."

"Go to hell," she shot back.

"Already been there. No thanks."

They left the building and went around to stand in front of Yvonne's fenced porch. The curtains were closed, but it was still easy to see where the telescope was probably focused. Bangers.

Suspicion flashed through Rafe and immediately Syndelle remembered an earlier conversation.

You were at Bangers, when you could have been anywhere else.

I was there because Brann ordered me to be there.

Why?

Who the hell knows with vampires?

Her mind touched Brann's just as Rafe's did, the mix of emotions in Rafe too complicated to untangle, though anger resonated in his words as he said, *You want to tell me what the fuck is going on?*

Irritation rippled back along the link as Brann answered Rafe's unspoken accusation with a rebuke of his own. *Do you think I would knowingly send you into a dangerous situation without warning you first? For all that you try my patience, Rafael, I have no desire to see you hurt or killed nor do I wish to collect more enemies by having to avenge you.*

Rafe bristled and amusement flashed through Syndelle along with the image of two large cats, their backs arched and their hair standing on end as they spit at each other. But when she shared her vision with her mates, they turned their scowling attention on her, the force of their regard rubbing against her like two prowling tigers and making her body grow heavy with the knowledge that passion of one kind could easily lead to passion of a different kind.

Later, Brann promised. His voice a purr that licked over her. His earlier irritation gone.

Why did you send Rafe to Bangers?

There have been a number of new slaves at Wyldfyres, faces I have seen in Rafe's memories of Bangers.

Syndelle's heart jerked, her stomach tightened and she felt a stab of quickly suppressed pain move through Rafael. *Wyldfyres?*

It was Rafe who answered, *Skye wondered if there was a place in Vegas where vampires go to fuck and feed in the company of other vampires. Wyldfyres is that place, though I have not been through its doors.*

And you wish to go? Brann challenged. *You, a companion who doesn't even offer his blood freely?*

Exasperation tangled with a mix of less easily identifiable emotions inside Syndelle. If she wasn't careful, her two mates were going to give her a headache that even a vampire's blood couldn't cure!

Do you think this has anything to do with the slaves from Bangers? she asked, once again redirecting Brann and Rafael's attention to the matter at hand.

It would seem likely, Brann said. From his mind she got a glimpse of the club with its theme of fire and its rooms designed for public sex and various forms of violence.

Syndelle shivered, wondering if her new mate enjoyed such entertainments, but she didn't ask.

What faces did you recognize? Rafe asked, and along the link, Syndelle sensed Brann's hesitation, his wariness, and wondered about it, especially when a heavy sigh escaped before he flipped through a number of images, all women that Rafe had fucked.

She stiffened, hurt by the images though she had no right to be. There had been plenty of men and women before her, she knew that, and yet…

None of them mattered to me, Rafe said, hugging her to him, and then asking Brann, *Who owns the new slaves?*

Syndelle felt Brann's shrug before she heard his words. *Minor vampires. None that I would give a second thought to, but given what you have found here, perhaps I need to check into it further.*

By going to the club? Syndelle couldn't stop herself from asking.

A phantom caress glided over her cheek and across her lips. *Do not upset yourself, Syndelle. I will feed only — and choose among the men available for such activity if you would prefer that I not touch another female — even as a source of food. I will do nothing more but take sustenance. There will be no other lovers for me except my Angelini mate and perhaps, one day, my presently reluctant companion.*

Skye's cell phone rang and she answered it, speaking only for a brief moment before saying, "That was Augustino. He's got someone lined up to put the temporary tattoo on Rafael."

They returned to the car, tossing around theories as to why a vampire slave was watching Bangers, but coming up with nothing that could be proved or disproved.

When they got to the police station, Skye said, "There's Augustino, I'll drop you guys here then park the car."

"Just Rafael," Syndelle said, opening the door and climbing out, her manner distracted, her hand clinging to the car door, a silent indication that she intended to get back in.

Uneasiness moved through Rafe, his own and Brann's. Neither of them wanted to let her out of their sight, and yet she was safe enough in front of the police station with her Angelini sister.

Rafe couldn't stop himself from hugging her briefly and saying, "See you in a few minutes," before moving away to join Augustino.

"What's up?" Skye asked when Syndelle got back in the car.

Syndelle turned so that she was facing Skye. "Is your mate listening?"

"Not anymore. He flickered out before I blocked him."

"I'd like you to take me to the strip and leave me there."

Alarm poured through Skye and it was all she could do to force the overwhelming emotion out of her body and mind. Shit! The memories she'd acquired of her family were great, but the compulsions involving Syndelle's safety were overpowering, almost smothering.

"Why do you want to go there?"

For a moment, uncertainty hovered around Syndelle, tempting her to confide in Skye. To tell her that finding the slave mark on Yvonne's door and the discussion of Wyldfyres had made the ancient power restless, impatient, that even now it pushed at Syndelle, as though it was suddenly anxious to escape. She shook her head. It wasn't Skye's burden to bear. It was hers. "I can't tell you what you want to know, only that I need some time alone." *To walk among the humans freely as I have been unable to do. To come to terms with what the freeing of the magic means for them.*

"The part that's *only me* wants to say yes," Skye said after a few minutes of silence. "But *that part* seems to be at war with every other part." She shook her head, trying to free herself from the inherited compulsions. No wonder Syndelle wanted some time alone! Leaving the care of their parents and brothers only to end up with Brann and Rafael was like never knowing a moment of freedom. And yet... Skye's heart raced and adrenaline surged through her system at the idea of leaving Syndelle on the Vegas Strip.

Syndelle said nothing, though the blood memories spoke volumes to Skye. Until the Angelini magic had kicked in and driven her to take Gian and Rico as her mates, Skye had been alone, but not lonely. She'd gone where she wanted to go, done what she wanted to do, proven her worth to herself and to those who had hired her to find the missing. She'd been her own person, taken risks and suffered the consequences or gained the reward. She'd lived.

Her sister's life had been the complete opposite. From the day of her birth she'd been protected and guarded, at first because she was female and their parents couldn't bear the thought of losing another daughter, and then later Syndelle and their brother Niall had been attacked by rogue werewolves after sneaking away from the compound. Somehow they'd managed to survive the attack, but the protection surrounding Syndelle had intensified. Here the memories were blurry and Skye assumed this was when their parents determined that Syndelle would never be a hunter.

Skye shrugged off the feeling that there were things about her sister that she didn't understand. She sighed, knowing there was probably going to be hell to pay over this, but Skye pulled the car away from the curb and headed toward the strip.

Chapter Thirteen

Syndelle moved through the crowds of people, opening herself to their thoughts and feelings as she tried to imagine what it was like to live as they did.

Their lives were short movies on a screen that spanned centuries. And yet in so many ways they had more choices than one born Angelini.

The ancient magic that created the Angelini also gave them a preordained destiny. They had always been hunters, law enforcers, guardians who helped keep the supernatural beings in check. And while the Angelini could choose where they lived, how they hunted, sometimes even what they considered to be justice—there was no choice in who they would mate with, no choice in *what* they would become.

Part of her wanted to turn away from her destiny—at least for a while. To ignore her mates in favor of exploring this human world and experiencing the freedom that came with choice. It was a heady temptation fueled by the powerful emotions of the humans around her—the intoxicating sensation that anything was possible in Vegas.

With a thought, she could tell that Rafael was safe, guarded by Detective Augustino, protected by Brann's magic, and to a lesser extent, her own. Nothing would happen to her mate while she yielded to temptation, free to explore for the first time in her life, free to pretend that her existence was no different than a human's. Putting off for a little while, the moment that was nearing. The moment when she would truly become *The Masada*. The vampire's myth turned into reality.

This night she would claim her freedom. This night she would taste what others took for granted, she would embrace it fully, knowing that it might be the only night she experienced it.

* * * * *

Brann prowled through the crowds of humans, casting his net and fishing through their minds for glimpses of Syndelle.

Rage and fear swirled inside him. It was one thing for Rafael to defy him, to take risks. He didn't worry that his often-troublesome companion could take care of himself. Beyond the hint of magic and the sheer lust that had first attracted him to Rafael, it was Rafe's ability to survive, his innate intelligence that had made him worth pursuing despite the aggravation Brann often experienced.

But Syndelle was another matter. He didn't need to see her memories to know how sheltered she'd been kept. Her family would never have allowed her to wander freely. Nor did he intend to allow her to do so once she was back in his possession.

He'd been too lenient with Syndelle just as he'd probably been too lenient with Rafael. But after being alive for so many centuries, time had become meaningless, something to be noted but not concerned with.

No longer. She was priceless to any vampire who could possess her. He couldn't risk losing her. He couldn't risk that she would fall into another's hands, or be destroyed by someone who understood just what she was.

The Masada.

He felt it in every cell of his body.

And though she fought her destiny, perhaps even doubted it, there was no escaping it. Some of the same ancient magic that flowed through her also flowed through him. Brann recognized her for what she was and she would never be free to escape him again.

She would be his companion, even if he had to take her to the point of death to make it so. Through her he would walk in the sunshine again. And through her, those of his blood might one day feel the sun on their faces as well.

He should have immersed himself in the entire gift that was Syndelle, instead of unwrapping and savoring it slowly. But she'd beguiled him, made him hesitate when he should have struck.

His thoughts touched Gian's and the others of his line, frustration making Brann dangerous, his temper growing shorter and his muscles tightening when he saw that none of them had found anything but fleeting evidence of Syndelle's passing.

A fitting punishment for one who so often advises his get on how to handle an Angelini mate, Gian said, his voice amused, though Brann could also feel Gian's underlying concern.

And were it not for your Angelini mate, then my own wouldn't be roaming free.

True, but perhaps now you more fully understand…

Brann snarled, *There is nothing to understand, other than the lesson that it is foolish to be controlled by your cock!*

Gian laughed. *Spoken by one who is newly mated. One, who for all his supposed wisdom, has not yet realized that each coupling with an Angelini mate only makes it more impossible to control them, not less.*

You will see that lie for what it is once I have Syndelle back in my possession.

Then I await the revelation with bated breath, Gian said, his amusement stronger than ever.

And once again, I see I have sired a disrespectful ass. One who makes me think of a promising harvest that has aged into vinegar instead of fine wine.

Ah, you crush me, Sire.

If only that were true, then perhaps I could remake you into a less aggravating son of my line.

An image flickered in Brann's mind and he dropped the link with Gian so he could focus on its source—a man who'd seen Syndelle, who'd tried to lure her to his bed. Brann's gums tingled as his fangs prepared to lengthen so that he could sink them into the human's throat and drain him of his lifeblood for daring to approach Syndelle.

That'd be really helpful, Rafael said, his mind joining with Brann's though they were miles apart. *Perhaps the council would even invite one of Syndelle's relatives to hunt you down for such an offense.*

Brann's snarl vibrated down the line between them. *Forget the search for this killer of humans, join me in looking for our missing Angelini mate.*

And risk that she'll show up in one of the places she knows I'm supposed to hunt tonight, while I'm not around to protect her? She's safer on the strip. Rafe showed Brann the view in front of him, the drunk men and the calculating and strung-out whores who serviced them. *Anything from the others looking for her?*

Nothing.

We'll find her. Or she'll come back to us, Rafe said, though his heart stuttered for a moment, and he almost wanted to feel the lash of Brann's temper so that his own guilt wouldn't continue to tear at him. He should never have let her out of his sight. But fuck, how was he to know…

Enough! Even I did not guess what she intended. Now she's gotten a taste of freedom and she rushes to embrace it. I can't fault her in that, though it will never happen again. You are blameless in this.

There was no way Rafe could hide his gratitude at hearing Brann's words. Emotion swelled inside him, sending warmth to his heart and blood to his cock. For the first time since Brann had saved his life, they had a cause they shared to the deepest part of their souls, something that bound them together and made them equals.

I can leave here, Rafael volunteered, wanting to demonstrate that finding Syndelle was more important to him than finding the man who'd killed Justin.

No, you were right. She may well come to the places she expects you to be. It would be unwise to entrust her safety to others. Even with her blocks, your body will know she is near, just as you know when I am near.

Rafe stiffened as an invisible hand stroked his cock, an intimate caress along the link he shared with Brann. He'd experienced it before, many times, but usually when Brann was frustrated and trying to prove a point, never like this, when there was a softer emotion between the two of them, a warmth that spoke of true companionship, a touch that both took and gave comfort.

A man bumped up against Rafe, drawing his attention back to his surroundings and immediately filling him with wariness at the sight of the vampire slave now leaning against the bar next to him.

"Well, if it isn't Brann's fuck-toy. Long time no see, Rafael."

"Not long enough, Frankie," Rafe said, looking at the man who'd lured him to Drac's and into Lilith's deadly trap.

A sweat-soaked human with silver studs outlining the shape of his mouth, took up a position on the other side of Rafael, moving into Rafael's space as though trying to provoke him into a fight.

"Back off," Rafe said.

The human grinned. "Or what? Your daddy will come beat me up?" He licked a stud-pierced tongue over his lips. "I'd like that. Does he give good pain?"

The human reached for Rafe and it was all he could do to allow the touch so that Brann's power could flow through him and explore the other man's mind. Filth poured in, blood-slick and dark, coating over an image that had been taken from Yvonne's mind when she'd opened her door and found Skye, Rafael and Syndelle standing there. But before Brann could push deeper, Frankie's fist slammed into his companion's face, sending him to the floor where he remained with blood pouring from his nose and leaking past his metal-studded lips. "Stupid fucker."

"Why are you here, Frankie?"

The other man smiled. "I heard a rumor that you were back to fucking girls. What's wrong? Brann not live up to your expectations? He such a pussy in bed that you'd rather have a cunt?"

Rafe touched his mind to Brann's. *What if I beat the shit out of him and find out what he knows at the same time?*

Brann's voice was sardonic. *As you said to me earlier, "That'd be really helpful." Leave him alone. Whatever game he's playing, he's doing so on another's orders.*

Rafael frowned, sensing that Brann didn't know who owned Frankie. *I thought he belonged to Lilith.*

No. When we saw him last, he was not anyone's slave. But Lilith would never form a blood-tie with someone like him. Even her slaves have descended from kings. Her companion, Ishana, was once revered as a minor goddess. Lilith would view the exchanging of even a single drop of blood with Frankie as wallowing in filth and allowing it to embrace her.

If I touched him, could you tell who he belonged to?

Perhaps. But he may well be a trap that neither of us wants to stumble into right now. Especially while Syndelle is unguarded.

Muscles knotted in Rafael's stomach at the mention of Syndelle. There were vampire politics swirling into play. Dangerous, deadly games that he wasn't sure Syndelle could survive.

He'd been with Brann long enough to know some of the rules and some of the players, but he knew very little about the Angelini hunters and even less about their females. Except for Skye and Syndelle, the few he'd met had always been clearly marked with a winged creature tattooed on their necks. They'd also been mated to vampires and had worn companion necklaces.

Syndelle had neither a tattoo nor a medallion to offer her protection. *Will she be safe if she encounters a vampire?*

A young vampire, yes. An ancient one, no.

Rafe's heart jerked in his chest. He tried to follow the trail of Brann's thoughts, to see why Brann was so sure that she wouldn't be safe, but there was a barrier, an impenetrable wall blocking the path. *You will learn soon enough, but it is safer for all of us if you don't know right now.* A small flash of humor offset the rebuff. *Though I am pleased to find you suddenly interested in the "fucking vampire politics" you have railed against for the last two years.*

Do I have a choice? Rafael growled out of habit.

As I have told you before. There are always choices.

As if death is an alternative.

Whether quick or slow, it is for many. The children you grew up with were taught to welcome it. You yourself were indoctrinated with such beliefs and yet you escaped.

Now it was Rafael's turn to slam his mind shut. To close off his memories of the cult that had spawned him. Rage swelled inside him. Despite all the successful witch and vampire hunts he'd accompanied Brann on, they'd never been able to find Diego or his band of perverted fanatics. They'd never been able to send them to the demon-infested hell where they belonged.

I will continue this hunt then, Rafe said.

And I will continue mine.

Along the bond, Rafe felt a hint of Brann's resolve to make Syndelle his companion. His implacable resolve that it *would* happen as soon as she was back in their possession.

I want to be there, Rafe said, knowing that being in the presence of so much magic, being a participant, would only tighten the leash he'd been fighting for the last two years.

It's your choice, Brann said — words that had Rafe gritting his teeth, fighting out of habit, though he knew that in Syndelle's presence he might finally yield to both his own and Brann's desires.

Chapter Fourteen

☙

The wolf shifted, the hair along its spine tingling, ready to stiffen with aggression at the first sign of a threat. Syndelle tensed and turned, searching for the source of the wolf's uneasiness and latching onto it immediately.

Ishana, the vampire companion from Rafael's memories, stood near the blackjack tables, her attention fixed on Syndelle. For a brief instant their eyes met, but the distance was too great, and Ishana's mind too well-guarded by her bond with Lilith for Syndelle to get even a glimmer of what the other woman was thinking.

Syndelle broke the contact and moved away, choosing caution over foolish confrontation. For a moment she was tempted to open the link with Brann.

The sun would rise soon. She could feel its power building even though the casino insulated its guests from the reality of the outside world. Despite the shields separating her mind from those of her mates, she could sense Brann's rage and frustration as he was forced to retreat. She could feel Rafe's worry as he left the club where he'd been hunting for his friend's killer. And for a moment the longing to be with her mates almost overwhelmed her desire for freedom.

As if sensing her weakness, Brann's voice rushed in, full of heavy compulsion and dark intent. *Return to the compound!*

She blocked him, but it was getting more difficult. Perhaps he had already gained from her blood—or perhaps it was the magic, weakening her so that her shields could be breached. So that Brann could take full possession.

Syndelle shivered, her thoughts turning to her own need for sanctuary. She was tired. Overstuffed with the thoughts and emotions of the humans she'd encountered.

Skye would welcome her, but she feared she'd already caused her newfound sister enough trouble. Guilt flowed in where earlier there had been a heady sense of excitement and adventure.

She'd acted selfishly when she'd asked Skye to help her escape the confines of her own destiny. Not only had she exposed Skye to Brann's wrath, but should their parents find one daughter only to lose another... Syndelle's heart lurched at what her flight might cost them all.

A prostitute sashayed past her as she left the casino, causing her thoughts to veer off to the girl she'd found in the alley. And in an instant, Syndelle knew that's where she would go.

Big Daddy had said he owed her a favor, and this was the favor she'd ask. Sanctuary for the day. And then she would return to her mates.

The wolf settled again, curling its body though it remained alert. The ancient magic inside Syndelle whispered like a breeze over a sunlit plain, though she knew in the space of a heartbeat it could howl like wind through a sacred canyon. It was calm now, as if finally her own course flowed with the course it had plotted.

She slipped into a taxi, catching the driver's eyes with hers when he looked into the rearview mirror. With her mind she showed him where she wanted to go, soothing away his instant fear with the promise that he would be safe. Reassuring him that he would be paid well for making the trip, even though he was to forget he'd ever taken her there as soon as she left the cab. He nodded, accepting the commands, then looking away, already only partially aware of the passenger in his cab.

Syndelle drew a ward on the back of the driver's seat when he pulled to a stop in front of Big Daddy's house. It flared to life, a protection that would last until he was finished working.

He didn't look toward the backseat, didn't say anything about what was due. Syndelle read the fare meter and counted out the money, placing it on the seat next to him and murmuring a soft command for him to keep the change before leaving the cab and watching him drive away.

Two men and several girls lounged on the front porch of Big Daddy's house. Syndelle recognized the men, but not the girls.

"I need a place to stay for the day," she told the man closest to her.

He nodded. "Go on in. Mama Jo already knows Big Daddy's granted you his protection."

Syndelle moved inside and was met almost instantly by a heavyset woman. "You here to see the new girl again?"

"Is she awake?"

The woman waved her arm. "Don't know. Go on back if you want to."

An image fluttered through Syndelle's mind. A picture of this woman standing in the doorway with Itai in the hallway behind her, of her blocking the way and saying that the girls weren't here. Skye's memory. It piqued Syndelle's curiosity. Her eyes met the woman's but the woman only snorted as a protection spell flared to life between them. "Don't try none of that shit on me. You want to find out something, you ask like anyone else and take whatever answer I give you."

Surprise ripped though Syndelle, followed by amusement and respect. "My brother was here."

The woman snorted again. "And I told him the same thing. Would have told the other one, too, Skye, but she had more sense than to try and mess with me."

Syndelle had seen Skye's earlier hunt for some missing girls when she'd meshed their palms together and mingled their blood. In truth, all of Skye's life had become part of Syndelle's blood-memory, though she would not violate her sister's privacy by examining the stored images. "I know what Skye wanted. What about Itai?" She wasn't sure whether to be relieved or worried that Itai's hunt might overlap the one she, and Skye, and Rafael were on.

Mama Jo shook her head. "Don't know what he was looking for. Sniffed around the house for a few minutes before Skye showed up, then for a few minutes after. Far as I could tell, he didn't find what he was looking for."

Syndelle cocked her head, letting her senses flair out in a gentle probe that didn't raise the protection spell, as she silently asked, *What are you?*

But there was no answer and Syndelle couldn't tell whether it was because the question wasn't heard or the woman in front of her refused to answer.

"Go on back now," Mama Jo said. "There's a cot set up in the room Wren's in. Nobody'll bother you if you need to sleep for a while, and there are some spare clothes in the closet. If you're hungry, come around to the kitchen and I'll fix you something to eat."

"Thank you," Syndelle said before moving to the back room and feeling strangely disappointed when she found Wren asleep. She stopped next to the bed, seeing again the girl's ruined face and painful injuries.

The magic inside Syndelle gathered and she knew it was the reason she'd heard Wren's call for help. The reason why she'd been drawn here when she could easily have found shelter in a hotel room. The magic wanted something from this beaten and scarred girl.

Even though Wren was covered with a sheet, in her mind's eye, Syndelle could see the coven mark branded above the girl's hip. What was Wren doing here? What was she running from? And where was her coven? The witches and warlocks who were bound to her by the pledges they'd made to one another. Why had they allowed this to happen to a young member of their circle?

No one chose this life. True, Big Daddy appeared to treat his girls well, but that didn't change the fact that they were prostitutes, hookers who trolled the streets and bars, accepting the attention of anyone with the money to pay for their services.

These weren't high-class call girls, the nature of their trade masked in glamour and money. These were runaways and junkies, the desperate who sold their bodies for shelter and food and the illusion of being part of a family—for protection or at least the knowledge that their deaths would be avenged.

Syndelle frowned. Was that why Wren was here? Had she sensed the graveyard magic surrounding Big Daddy and thought he might be her only hope of surviving?

She eased the sheet down, horrified once again by the brutality the girl had suffered, by the sight of the word *whore* carved into her stomach. Syndelle stopped when the brand and the pentacles were exposed.

The ancient magic swirled to life. This young witch was important to it. It had a purpose for her—separate from Syndelle—and yet it could touch the girl only through Syndelle.

Syndelle closed her eyes so that she could concentrate on what was wanted of her. So that she could fight against it if she thought it necessary.

From the moment her parents had discovered how different she was from their other children, they'd done their best to train her, to help her cope with the old power that flowed through her body, the ancient blood memories that remembered a time when vampires walked in daylight and magic ruled the land. It was a primordial force that saw the world in terms of millenniums, accepting that chaos and devastation in one century would ultimately lead to rebirth and growth in another century.

From death came new life. From the destruction of one people came new civilizations. It was an endless circle in which the individual meant nothing.

Syndelle shivered. Feeling the weight of responsibility. Knowing that to unleash any of the magic was like throwing a stone in a pond and watching it ripple outward without being able to guess all the places it would ultimately touch.

But the promise to heal this girl whispered through Syndelle's mind. The magic would take away her pain and restore her—if Syndelle allowed some of it to escape her body. It was her choice. Her gift. Her destiny.

Syndelle touched a fingertip to the brand mark, drawing blood as she bit her lip in order to keep from crying out as she experienced the searing heat of iron against flesh—as she was absorbed in the darkness of the girl's memories and felt the girl's panicked need to escape something so evil that it had terrified her, first sending her to drugs and then to the streets in a effort to hide from it.

Syndelle tried to push deeper, to see what had scared Wren, but the way was blocked, the spells keeping the secret locked away, tainted and vile.

The wolf stood, its hackles raised, though rather than attack, it cautiously took a step back, pulling Syndelle's mind from the girl's as it did so.

Shaken, Syndelle wanted to bury her face in the wolf's ruff and seek protection from the evil she'd brushed against. It was an evil similar to the one she'd felt once before, when she and Niall had been attacked by the rogue werewolves outside their family's compound.

Her heart pounded in her chest as the memories of that day flew through her mind, immersing her in terror and horror, and for a second she stared at her hands, remembering the moment when she'd clawed herself out of the all-consuming darkness and endless silence, when she'd looked down and seen the blood on her hands and the dead bodies of the Weres at her feet. Slashed by talons that had erupted from the tips of her fingers, torn to shreds when the blood connection with Sabin had allowed him to take her place in the sun and use her body to kill.

She shuddered, remembering that first experience in the abyss, how she'd known instinctively that if she couldn't escape that ancient place, then she would become a part of it, absorbed as others had been in the past, while it waited for another to be born, one who was strong enough to both contain it and wield it.

Syndelle forced the old memories aside. Forced back the need to seek comfort and protection. If she was to take her place, then she couldn't remain forever sheltered and guarded from the things that would test and possibly harm her. She couldn't avoid the decisions and choices that were hers to make.

She took her finger off the brand and gathered the blood that had escaped when she bit her lip, signing in the air the ancient symbols necessary to protect herself before touching her fingers to Wren and tracing the coven mark, letting the magic flow into the sleeping girl, watching as the brand darkened to the color of old blood.

When it was done, Syndelle pulled the sheet back over the girl and moved to the cot, curling up in its center, allowing herself to be warmed and guarded by the wolf as she sought the comfort of sleep.

Almost immediately Brann appeared, a strong presence moving along the boundaries of her shield like a tiger pacing the perimeter of another's territory and looking for a place to enter. Syndelle smiled in her sleep and dropped enough of her guard so that they could be together, but not so much that he could find her.

He didn't come bounding right in, but instead studied the situation cautiously, and in the process, unknowingly gave her confidence a boost. She would be able to handle this mate!

Rafael's presence joined Brann's in a smooth blending that had Syndelle's heart filling with warmth and anticipation. Something had happened between the two men, something had shifted and changed between them and the feel of their harmony made her womb flutter and her body swell with the desire to go to them, to be with both of them.

Tell us where you are and Rafael will come and get you, Brann whispered, his voice soft and compelling. An ancient vampire's voice meant to be obeyed.

She laughed, glad that he was testing her, that he wasn't so sure of her weakness that he didn't bother to try and use the force of his will on her. *I'll come to you at the end of the day. I'm safe where I am.*

The compulsion intensified, strengthened by the Angelini bond and the blood she'd shared with him. But still she was able to resist his command.

Let me come and get you, Rafael pleaded, letting her feel the tension in his body. *I've been up all night trying to find the killer. Don't make me sleep alone.*

For a moment she weakened, wanting to feel his body against hers, wanting to feel his cock plunging in and out of her as his teeth locked onto her shoulder. The wolf stirred, its body also heavy with desire. It was willing to return to Brann's home. It was willing to give up the last hours of freedom in order to mate.

Syndelle wavered, torn between the current demands of her heart and body and her earlier resolve. But Brann tipped the scale by choosing that moment to strengthen his command that she reveal where she was.

No. I will see you this evening. That will be soon enough, she said, immediately blocking out the sounds of their protest, though she stayed connected to them so that they would know she was safe, and she would know the same about them.

Chapter Fifteen
ɞ

It was a little more than an hour away from sunset when Syndelle made her way into the mostly gay bar where Rafael was hunting. She'd thought to return to Brann's compound earlier, but sleep had held her in its grip — or the magic had — not releasing her until the turmoil in Big Daddy's house had finally penetrated, waking her to a flurry of activity and the sight of Wren's empty bed.

"Where is she?" Syndelle asked as she rolled off the cot, glad that she'd left her clothes on now that the room held several of Big Daddy's men.

"You didn't see her leave?" one of them asked, his face full of suspicion.

"No."

"She say anything to you?"

"She never woke up."

In the hallway a girl said, "I swear I saw her! She even turned around when I yelled her name. She looked like she always looked, like nothing had happened to her. It was Wren! Who else would have been running along the railroad tracks?"

"Go on to bed," Mama Jo said. "You're imagining things, now you've got these other girls all stirred up. You got Angel and Tia upset."

"But—" There was a sound of flesh hitting flesh. A slap.

"Go on now. Do what I said. If you saw someone running along the tracks, it wasn't that girl."

But it had been.

Syndelle followed the girl's trail down to the railroad tracks, the wolf enjoying the hunt until Big Daddy's black limousine pulled up alongside her, forcing her to stop. "Get in," he said, opening the door from the inside. When she took a seat, he said, "Don't worry about the girl. She doesn't owe Big Daddy anything. She's free to go her own way. Plenty more around to take her place. Always plenty more." He leaned back in his seat, his aura brushing against Syndelle's as he studied her. "Big Daddy heard a rumor that Skye was your sister. Any truth to that rumor?"

"Yes."

"Thought you told Big Daddy that you only had a brother here. Thought you told Big Daddy that you didn't know his friend Skye."

"I didn't know she was my sister when I told you that. I hadn't met her yet."

His cobra eyes stared at her for a long moment, and then he nodded slightly. "Blood always tells. Blood never forgets. Big Daddy don't want no trouble—not with Skye or the Lady Syndelle." He pressed a key on the console next to his hand, telling the driver to go to The Hole, before telling Syndelle, "Rafe is there along with your sister. I figure that's where you want to be, too."

Syndelle nodded, and a few minutes later she found Skye sitting at a table, watching as several men hit on Rafael. "Anything?" she asked, the wolf's low growl telling Syndelle that it didn't enjoy the sight of other men propositioning its mate any more than it had liked seeing him surrounded by Roman's flock of human sheep.

"Nothing." Skye grinned. "But it's good to see you."

"I shouldn't have involved you. I'm sorry."

Skye surprised Syndelle by reaching across the table and taking her hand, making the blood in their veins hum with comfort and solidarity. "Don't be. Involve me anytime." She gave a wry smile. *Just show me that ward for blocking out Brann and Gian first. The inside of my head still feels a little scorched.*

Syndelle laughed. *I'll teach you some wards. Or our mother will. She's a powerful sorceress, as was her mother before her. It's a rare talent among the Angelini.*

Skye's heart jumped at the mention of their mother, at the prospect of being reunited with a family she would never have imagined as belonging to her. "When will they be here?"

"I don't know." *It is not often that the Angelini gather as they are doing now.* A small knot of dread formed in Syndelle's stomach. Had some of the oldest among them felt the rise in the old magic, somehow sensing that the ancient power had found a way to return? She shivered, knowing that her parents had always feared the day might come when *she* would be hunted. When they might have to kill hunters they'd fought side by side with in order to protect her.

The wolf turned its attention away from Rafe and brushed against Syndelle's soul in a gesture of comfort. *You worry needlessly. Perhaps if you were unmated, there would be those foolish enough to turn against the Coronado line, even knowing that Riesen's old pack would join with the Coronados in a fight to the death. But soon all will know of your existence, and when they do, they will know you have claimed Brann for your mate. None of the governing councils would dare to wage war against the wolves, the Coronados, those of Brann's line and all of their allies. It would be like one of the humans' civil wars, where even the victors are losers.*

Syndelle closed her eyes, in her mind gently brushing her cheek against the soft fur of the wolf. *Where would I be without you?*

The wolf snapped its teeth together, its eyes sparkling with amusement. *Perhaps you'd be almost as pathetic as one of these humans—one of which is getting ready to lose a hand if he continues to try and grope our mate.*

Syndelle laughed, as the wolf had intended she would. *Remind me not to ask that question again,* she told it as she opened her eyes and saw that one of the men who'd been talking to

Rafael had moved closer—too close in both the wolf and Syndelle's opinion.

Rafe switched his beer from one hand to the other and Skye said, "That's the signal that this guy is giving Rafael the creeps. You want to do the honors of checking him out, or should I?"

"I'll do it," Syndelle said, rising immediately.

Skye grabbed Syndelle's wrist before she could stalk over to the bar. *Don't blow his cover! You can hit on him, or just buy yourself a drink while you check out the guy giving him the creeps, but try not to let on that you and Rafe are a couple.*

Syndelle stood for a long moment, at war with herself, at war with the wolf, until finally the wolf grumbled, wanting to rip into the man standing too close to Rafe, but reluctantly settling with the knowledge that Syndelle would order him away from Rafe if he wasn't the one they sought.

Brann hadn't lied. As soon as Syndelle had arrived, Rafe's cock had hardened into an unbearable rod of pain— unfortunately sending the wrong message to the men who'd been hitting on him. Fuck. Had he ever really thought that this scene was fun? Challenging? Amusing?

Yeah. He had, once, a long time ago, though in the end it had become a lifestyle, a survival method, something he did out of habit because he didn't know anything else or have anywhere else to go.

But now he had Syndelle and he hated for her to see him like this, even though he knew she accepted that it had to be done if they were going to find Justin's killer. Rafe tensed as she rose from her seat, the wolf so obvious in her body posture that he wasn't sure whether she'd hypnotize the creep who wouldn't take no for an answer, or tear him to shreds.

When Skye grabbed Syndelle's arm, Rafe relaxed, allowing his heart to experience the warmth of Syndelle's caring. And then Syndelle was there, her voice seductive as she called the man's attention to her with a question. "Do you two want a third for your little party?"

There was no resistance in the man. He fell into Syndelle's eyes and filled her mind with his fantasies of locking Rafe's wrists and ankles to an odd piece of furniture, then taking a whip to her mate's back and buttocks before fucking him. The wolf snarled in reaction, flashing its teeth before Syndelle could prevent it and the man's fantasies faded, replaced by the terror of a prey animal that has been cornered by a predator. Syndelle could hear his heart racing and the wolf wallowed in the smell his fear.

The wolf held him at bay as Syndelle pushed deeper into his thoughts, shuffling through his memories like a deck of cards, following any thread that might prove he was the one they were looking for. But as much as the wolf would have liked him to be, he wasn't.

With a final command to give up his pursuit of Rafael, Syndelle blinked and freed the man from her gaze. He turned away almost immediately and stumbled toward the men's room.

"Guess he wants a different kind of action," Rafe joked, and when Syndelle's eyebrows drew together he flashed a picture of the bathroom in this particular bar, the stall doors fitted with holes large enough for even the most well-endowed man to stick his cock through. *For guys who like a little danger with their blowjobs*, Rafe added, enjoying her surprise. *I take it that none of your brothers ever shared this knowledge with you?* he teased, enjoying her laughter along their bond before she purchased a drink and retreated to Skye's table.

Despite the flirting, the catcalls and purchases of lap dances, there was a frantic desperation among the people in The Hole. "Is it always like this?" Syndelle asked, watching as new admirers flocked to Rafael.

"He's got something. Even when Brann's around, they still hit on him."

Syndelle wrinkled her nose and laughed. "Not my mate." She waved her hand to encompass the entire scene. "This."

"Yeah. Underneath it's always like this." She checked her watch. "We'll hang here for about thirty minutes more, then hit the next spot right around sunset." *Rico will take over and Augustino will jump to the third club on the list, just in case our killer is smart enough to worry about a trap.*

There was a commotion at the entrance and both women turned to look. Syndelle could feel Skye's dismay at the rough, leather-and-chain-clad men who'd entered. Out of the corner of her eye, she saw Detective Augustino move from a darkened area of the club to lean against the bar, positioning himself in case there was trouble. And from the aura of menace radiating off the men, Syndelle thought there would be.

Her gaze shifted to Rafe. *If a fight starts, you and Skye get out of here*, he said. *Have her take you home. It's almost sunset.*

"Get ready," Skye said. "As much as I'd like to stay and participate, Gian's burning up the airwaves with some heavy-duty compulsion. If something happens, we'll head for the door." Skye grimaced. "Like a bunch of other people who don't want to be part of this show. This is not exactly a fighting crowd."

Syndelle frowned, looking around at the predominantly gay and bisexual crowd. Patrons who definitely favored spandex and flashy dress over grunge or Goth, or the heavy leather and chains of the men who'd just entered. *If we could get in front of them, we could—* But before the sentence was complete, one of the men grabbed a waiter and tossed him into a table of club patrons, knocking drinks and chairs and people to the floor.

Screams and shouts followed, along with a rush to the door—or the fight. Skye grabbed Syndelle's wrist. "Let's go."

Syndelle looked for Rafe, but already he was lost amid the shoving and swearing and flailing. His voice and Brann's pushed at her mind, demanding that she get out of the club. She didn't resist Skye's urging and they joined the crush of bodies trying to escape the violence.

When they cleared the door they saw three additional men dressed in leather and chains waiting outside. *I don't like the looks of this*, Skye said, wariness flooding the link between them. *It feels like the guys inside are trying to flush someone out. Rafe and I came in Augustino's car and I don't have a key. Let's head to the right. We can duck into the card room at the corner.*

As soon as they broke away from the other fleeing patrons, the three men closed in on them and two others joined, stepping out of the shadows of the card room, effectively trapping Skye and Syndelle. *I guess we know who they were trying to flush out*, Skye said.

Bile rose in Syndelle's stomach as she felt the ancient magic swelling. As her fingertips itched, ready for the poison-filled talons to emerge. In the distance Brann's power surged, willing her to retreat to the abyss, to submerge herself in the deep silence and darkness, so that he could take her place, could fill her body like a hand fills a glove so thin that it's almost nonexistent.

But the wolf kept him out and the magic did not yield to him. Destiny whispered through her mind, it was time for *her* to take *her* place, for *her* to prove that she was a worthy vessel, a true Angelini—though one who was unlike any of the others.

A switchblade appeared in Skye's hand. *Do you have a weapon on you?*

Only myself. And I am untested.

There was no chance to escape the attack. No chance to retreat or run. Skye's blade flashed in the dim streetlights, sending one man reeling backward, cursing and grasping at a blood-drenched arm as another lunged forward. The other three had all gone for Syndelle, not hitting her as she'd anticipated but grabbing at her and trying to drag her away.

Her fear spiked and with it came the tearing pain of clear fingernails elongated into catlike claws. She fought, slashing wildly and finally connecting first with one of her attackers and then a second. They cursed, calling her a bitch and promising they were going to make her sorry, but within seconds they were screaming in agony, writhing and rolling on the ground, their arms and legs flailing as though they were on fire.

The three remaining men were momentarily distracted by their fallen friends and Skye took advantage, sending her blade home, through leather and flesh, straight into the heart of the attacker she slashed earlier. He crumpled in a heap and the other two panicked. "Fuck, forget about taking her, just kill her!" one yelled, pulling out a gun and aiming at Syndelle.

The bullet slammed into her chest. A painful burst of heat and power that sent her backward.

Her heart beat wildly, pouring blood through the opening as Brann and Rafe's screams filled her mind, sounding far away, as though a thick layer of ice stood between her and them. The wolf howled and spun in panic, clawing to remain in sunlight and noise as the infinite blackness and endless silence rushed up to claim Syndelle.

Stop!

From somewhere, nowhere, everywhere, the timeless voice that had always existed within Syndelle commanded, just as icy fingers closed around her heart and it ceased to beat.

Chapter Sixteen

Rafael carried Syndelle into Brann's bedroom, his face still wet from the tears he'd shed when he thought she was dead. Fuck. He'd never known so much pain, so much guilt.

What he'd experienced in those seconds before Brann told him that she'd somehow done what only vampires could do, somehow shut down her heart in order to preserve a small spark of life deep within her, surpassed even the haunting guilt of his escape from Diego's cult. His pain at knowing that the ones he'd left behind — the ones he didn't dare try to take with him for fear that they'd betray him before he could escape — would die. The boy children first, and then the girls — unless Diego had a "vision" and spared some of them by turning them into his wives or male concubines.

"Take her into the bathroom," Brann said and Rafael did so, reluctantly placing the bloody bundle that was Syndelle onto a blanket that Brann had spread across the luxurious room with its sunken tub. Together they stripped her of her clothing.

Rafe shivered, horrified at how pale and cold she was, how dead she seemed. One of Brann's fingernails extended into a claw and he opened a wound on his wrist, deep enough so that the blood flowed, a small stream that ran over his palm and down his fingers. He used the blood to trace symbols on the spots they'd both marked Syndelle as belonging to them — her neck, over her heart, her inner thigh — and the Angelini bond hummed to life, though her heart remained still.

Brann moved to the wound on her chest, filling the opening with his blood. Rafe's heart jumped, awed by the sight of her skin knitting back together. Without being told, he gently eased her over onto her stomach, exposing the horrifying damage the bullet had done when it left Syndelle's body. Once again, Brann filled the opening with his blood, and once again her body responded by healing, by knitting together as though she'd never been shot.

And yet she remained still and cold.

Brann licked across the wound on his wrist, closing it before standing and stripping out of his clothing, his cock full and heavy. Rafe cringed at the sight, vivid imagination and horrifying reality colliding, until Brann's rough purr of laughter washed over him. *True, the lure of fucking one who seems to be a corpse draws some vampires and their companions together, but that is not my intention here. I merely intend to take Syndelle into the bath I prepared for her, and see no reason to be uncomfortable. Do you join us?*

You could have warned me, Rafe grumbled, amused laugher welling up in his chest, easing the horrible tightness that had been a vise around his heart since the moment he'd felt Syndelle's death along the link.

He stood and stripped as Brann scooped Syndelle into his arms and settled into the sunken tub with her. Then he joined them, immersing himself in the hot water, assisting Brann as they both cleaned the blood from Syndelle's body while her temperature slowly rose.

It was the wolf that returned first, thrashing wildly in the first seconds when Syndelle's heart began beating and her lungs gasped for air. Syndelle followed, distant and weak from loss of blood, unable to do more than brush against her mates with her mind in order to reassure them.

Once again Brann's fingernail extended to a claw, but this time he slashed a wound on his chest and pressed Syndelle's lips to it, giving her his lifeblood until Rafe sensed that she had completely returned from wherever her spirit had retreated, though her eyes remained closed and her body was heavy with sleep as they left the bath, drying her and placing her on the bed.

Rafael stood next to Brann, so close that their shoulders touched. He couldn't take his eyes off the steady rise and fall of Syndelle's chest. Fuck. He never wanted to go through that again. Never. He was almost afraid to look away, even though he knew she was safe, alive.

He could feel Brann's emotions, his joy that she was still theirs, his rage that someone had tried first to take her, then to kill her. He also felt Brann's unswerving commitment to hunt down whoever was behind the attack. And underneath it all, Rafe felt Brann's need for blood, his gnawing hunger from having used his own resources to restore Syndelle.

"You need to feed," Rafe said, shifting his hair from one side to the other, silently, willingly offering his blood to Brann— the first time he'd done so since becoming Brann's companion.

When Brann didn't react to his offer, Rafael tilted his head and mocked, "Do I have to say the words? That I'm offering of my own free will?"

Brann laughed, a rich sound that wrapped itself around Rafe's cock and made him want to go to his hands and knees. "Far be it for me to turn down a suddenly willing companion. Kneel on the bed next to Syndelle."

Rafe shivered as he knelt, anticipating the moment when Brann's naked body was going to touch his, when Brann's cock would be trapped between the two of them.

In front of him, Syndelle's eyelids fluttered open, her gaze going almost instantly from cloudy confusion to smoky desire as she took in the sight of her two mates.

Rafe groaned when she rose to her knees, pressing the front of her body to his, kissing him first before licking over the place where both she and Brann had already marked him. He buried his face in the silky thickness of her hair and wrapped his arms around her, feeling the press of Brann's body as the vampire's arms enfolded both of his companions.

"You're okay?" Rafe whispered.

"Yes." Her lips found his again, their tongues meeting in a gentle twine of comfort and love before she pulled back and touched her mouth to Brann's, accepting the powerful thrust of his tongue, yielding to him as he communicated his intention to finish binding her to him.

When the kiss ended, Syndelle returned to Rafe's neck, gently biting before shifting out of the way so that Brann could feed. Rafe gave a sharp moan of protest and pleasure when she moved back even further just as Brann's fangs pierced his flesh and sent a jolt of exquisite sensation to his cock.

Syndelle's hands stroked down Rafe's chest, exploring the tight male nipples, playing with the ruby-tipped barbell and making him cry out. She leaned in, laving a tiny point, kissing and sucking until he was pleading for her to move lower, to put her mouth on his cock.

She pulled back then, sinful temptation and unspoken promise in her eyes as her hands found Brann's, urging them onto Rafael's body.

Rafe tensed, closing his eyes even as he accepted the need, the intensely erotic feel of firm, masculine hands moving across his abdomen, stroking downward to a cock that hungered for the hard, firm feel of another man's fingers, to testicles that were already pulled up tightly against his body.

There was no way he could hold back the moan of pleasure, the pre-cum that escaped as soon as Brann's fingers circled his cock, pumping, building the pleasure while his other hand grasped Rafe's testicles.

Syndelle's mouth and tongue left a wet trail of painful need behind as she followed Brann's path, stopping to explore Rafe's belly button before taking everything in front of Brann's hand into her mouth.

Rafael bucked against the twin pleasures, spearing his fingers in Syndelle's hair and holding her to him as his heart thundered in his chest and his lungs labored for air. He wanted to come in her mouth. He wanted to put her on her back and sink into her cunt as Brann sank into his ass.

Brann's hold on him tightened, pulling liquid fire through his body, from Rafe's cock to the spot where Brann's lips and fangs touched his skin. It was more pleasure than Rafael could ever have imagined feeling.

He bucked and shivered, crying out as Syndelle sucked harder, her wet mouth reducing him to pleading, Brann's hold on his testicles the only thing preventing him from coming, from releasing in Syndelle's mouth.

Your choice, Rafael, what do you want? Brann said as his fangs retracted.

You. Both of you.

Syndelle gave a last, lingering pull on his cock before moving away, her look sultry as she positioned herself on her back and spread her legs, exposing plump, wet cunt lips to her mates.

The sight of her female flesh almost undid Rafe, and he fell over onto his hands and knees, hovering above her with Brann's hand still on his cock, afraid that he wouldn't last more than a stroke inside her, that he'd scream like a virgin when Brann impaled him.

"Easy," Brann whispered as he pressed kisses along Rafe's spine. "In a minute we will be as one."

The hand that had been cupping Rafe's testicles dropped to Syndelle's body and trailed through her glistening slit, gathering her arousal and transferring it to Rafe, lubricating the tight pucker of his ass, preparing him.

Rafe cried out, shaking with need and turning to Syndelle for succor, closing the distance between his lips and hers, burying his tongue in the wet depths of her mouth as Brann's fingers worked in and out of his back entrance.

Now, Brann said, releasing his hold on Rafael's cock, and like a homing pigeon, it found Syndelle's sheath, plunging all the way in on the first stroke and holding steady there, waiting for Brann, acknowledging that in this, Brann would lead.

He cried out in painful pleasure as Brann's cock began penetrating him, as he slowly worked himself into a place that hadn't known another man since the night Rafe had become a companion. When Brann was all the way in, Syndelle's legs wrapped around the two men, holding them to her even as both she and Brann cradled Rafael between them. "Please," she whispered, her body heavy with lust, with the wolf's need to mate, with the Angelini magic rising in anticipation of what was to come.

Brann began pumping then, moving into Rafe's body, controlling Rafe's strokes into Syndelle, the bond between the three of them wide open so that the pleasure was magnified beyond what only one could feel. So that their cries were in concert, their movements perfectly synchronized in a dance that had existed from the beginning of time, in a dance that shattered over them in pleasure so exquisite that it was almost painful, so intense that it left them holding each other, fevered, sweat-slick skin pressed together as the magic engulfed them, swirling them downward until there was nothing but dark ecstasy.

Chapter Seventeen

∽

It was Syndelle who woke first, the sound of the doorbell and Skye's psychic demand for entry pressing the last of the magic-induced sleep from her mind. She mumbled, sending a message to Skye that her summons had been heard, as she tried to disentangle herself from Rafe's arms.

He tightened his hold on her, only waking when she continued to try and move out of his arms, when his penis slid from her channel, already half-hardened. "Shit," he said, releasing her and rolling to his back, rubbing his chest as he slowly woke up, his wild mane of hair and lazy sprawl making Syndelle think of the wolf.

"Skye is at the gate," Syndelle said, scrambling from the bed and moving to Brann's closet, quickly dressing before hurrying to greet her sister.

With a thought she touched Brann's mind and knew that he'd anticipated Skye's need to ensure herself that Syndelle was well, and had adjusted the wards so that Skye would have no trouble entering or leaving the compound. She could also feel his determination that as soon as the sun set again, he would claim her completely — whether she fought him or not. He *would* make her his companion, as he'd intended to do the night before, had the magic not held him in its grip, freeing him with only enough time to shower and seek his daytime resting place.

The sun struck Syndelle's skin and she wanted to lift her face to it in the same way the wolf liked to lift its face to the moon. Even knowing what freeing the magic would ultimately mean to the humans, to those who hunted the rogue vampires, could she really deny Brann that which he desired more than anything else?

Not more than anything else, Syndelle. I would not exchange your life for a chance to walk in the sun's rays.

Her heart raced while her mind tried to measure the truth in his words. He was her mate, chosen for her by the magic and the wolf—but for all that, he was still an ancient vampire.

And yet...a small, feminine smile played over Syndelle's lips. It had not been a vampire commanding her home yesterday when she'd explored the human world. It had been an irate mate, a worried husband.

When the sun sets, I will return to the house and become your companion, she said.

Like a wave trying to knock down an unwary beachcomber, Brann's will washed over Syndelle, his command forceful. *You will not leave the compound!*

Alone, Syndelle modified, arriving at the gate and tapping the keys so that Skye could stride in and swallow her in a fierce hug.

"I think it's time for you to teach me that ward," Skye said, unable to keep herself from tightening her arms around Syndelle in a second hug before releasing her. "Gian is suddenly far too present in my head."

Rafe joined them a moment later, wearing nothing but jeans, his golden hair and tanned skin glowing in the afternoon light. "What happened after I left with Syndelle?" he asked, wrapping his arms around Syndelle and pulling her back against his front.

"Damage control. Gian and some of the other vampires from Fangs came over to help Detective Augustino handle the fallout." She cocked her head. "I take it vampires and werewolves don't always play very nicely together."

Rafe grinned. "Too true. Were they able to learn anything?"

"No. No ID on the dead men. I even went down to the biker bar near Big Daddy's house to see if anyone knew the guys who'd attacked us. Not a fun group of minds to look into, but none of the men last night were familiar to any of the guys who hang out at the bar."

Rafe rubbed his cheek against Syndelle's soft hair. "It may be coincidence—not that I believe in them when it comes to vampires—but the first night I went trolling for our killer, a guy I knew in LA showed up. His name's Frankie. He's a vampire's slave now. He knew about Syndelle. And he was with a strung-out human who knew about our visit to Yvonne's room. When he touched me, Brann saw it in his mind. But before he could see more, Frankie punched the guy and knocked him out."

"I also saw someone from your past, and Brann's," Syndelle said. "Yesterday when I was wandering in the casinos." She flashed the memory of Ishana and felt Brann's immediate suspicion that the vampire Lilith was behind the attack.

"Fucking vampire politics," Rafe growled, fury filling his face. He'd once thought that Lilith was driven by lust and spite, wanting to punish Brann for turning down her overtures—but in the last two years Rafe had come to see Lilith for what she was, an ancient with a greedy, insatiable desire for power.

"Then maybe I need to pay another visit to Yvonne," Skye said.

Rafael rubbed his cheek against Syndelle's hair. "And Toppers. The human with Frankie would be drawn to a place like that. As long as he isn't a slave, he's still fair game if we can find him." Rafe smirked at Skye. "Unless your mates have forbidden you to hunt at Toppers after your last visit."

Skye scowled in response. "Rico and Gian know better than to try that. I'll check out Toppers."

"We," Syndelle said, her fingers gracefully tracing a series of symbols in the air and blocking out the immediate protests of both vampire mates. "We will check it out together."

Skye grinned. "That is definitely one handy ward."

Syndelle smiled. "It won't last long, only long enough for our mates to gain control of their tempers and remember that they are dealing with Angelini and not with helpless sheep who wish to do nothing but donate blood and obey a master."

Skye's eyes widened before she started laughing. Rafe's arms tightened around Syndelle. "Let Skye and I go while you stay here."

She turned in his arms, her heart melting at the agony she saw in his eyes, at the fear for her safety that vibrated through his body. *It will be okay. Even if Lilith was behind the attack, she will think her minions succeeded in killing me. She can't know for certain that I am anything other than human — a female that you and Brann have taken an interest in. I don't think anyone will be expecting us to retrace our steps. Especially so quickly.*

Brann...

She pressed her lips to Rafael's, sliding her tongue into his mouth and drawing a groan from his body as his cock filled and pressed against her. *I have promised Brann that I will yield to him at sunset. But I do not want my life to simply be a continuation of what it was when I was in the care of my parents and brothers. I do not want to be hidden behind walls, kept separate from the world around me. I will do nothing foolish, but I will not be left behind.*

Fear and need and respect struggled inside Rafe as he deepened the kiss, wanting nothing more than to return to bed and cover her with his body, tempting and teasing and pleasuring her until she locked his cock deep inside her, until the only world that existed was captured in an endless moment of shared ecstasy.

He dared to touch Brann's mind through the companion bond and found the vampire bombarded with the same emotions — though he sensed Brann's fear was multilayered, a complex struggle whose roots stretched across centuries. *Anytime you want to share the big secret about Syndelle with me, that would be great*, Rafe mocked, receiving a snarl in response before Brann growled, *Take her then. But she will be in my bed when the sun sets.*

Yes, oh master, I hear and obey, Rafe said and heard the echoes of Gian's laughter along the blood-tie with both Brann and the Coronado Angelini. He pulled away from Syndelle. "Let me finish getting dressed, then we can go."

As Rafe disappeared into the house, Skye studied her sister, reliving the horrible moments when she'd thought Syndelle was dead. Searching her blood-given memories for an explanation as to what had happened to the two men who'd attacked Syndelle and died so violently, screaming in agony from wounds that looked like shallow scratches.

Skye had been so busy fighting the other men that she hadn't seen much of Syndelle's struggle. *Do you have a weapon on you?* she'd asked before the attack came. *Only myself.*

Skye shook her head. Had she really been disappointed when she first saw Syndelle, thinking that her sister was as weak as one of the humans who flocked to Fangs? It seemed so obvious now that Syndelle was so much more...and yet so different than what Skye had come to think of as Angelini.

She is different, a voice whispered through Skye, and the wolf she was still becoming accustomed to rose within her, opening its eyes and staring at Syndelle. *She is* The Masada. *The foundation on which the old magic will return and build.*

Masada. The word fluttered at the edge of Skye's consciousness, elusive, and yet familiar, though some instinct warned that to mention the word out loud would be the same as summoning danger to her sister.

Skye concentrated, trying to more fully separate herself from the wolf, guessing that the knowledge that she herself couldn't reach, would live in the spirit-animal that she'd inherited from Riesen. *If I'm to keep her safe, I need to understand*, she directed to the wolf.

It laughed, a disconcerting feeling that made Skye shiver and frown, uncertain whether she really liked this latest development. It was bad enough having Gian and Rico in her head sometimes, not to mention Brann when he was in a rage and used the link he had with Gian, but this...

And yet...through the memories she now possessed, Skye recognized Riesen in this wolf. Riesen who often laughed and teased, who loved deeply and fiercely, who would kill without remorse if necessary, but would nip at heels and jump crazily at falling leaves just to make his children and mate laugh.

You are right, the wolf said, brushing along the inside of Skye as though it was stretching and filling every part of her. *If you are to help keep her safe then you must understand what she is, what it means to be* The Masada, *the one whose body is a chalice, whose blood is the elixir that can allow a vampire to walk in the sunlight. She is vampire myth made real, and though the myth varies depending on who is doing the telling, one part of it remains unchanged. The blood sacrifice of* The Masada *will bring an end to the days when all vampires are banished to the night.*

Skye's heart thundered in her chest. Blood sacrifice? Did that mean that her sister was destined to die?

Only if we can't keep her safe.

* * * * *

Even without Rafael sharing the memory of Skye being shot at Toppers, Syndelle could see why her sister's mates might try and keep her from visiting the club. It was a rough, dangerous place full of unclean, substance-ridden bodies that vibrated with violence and lack of restraint.

The three of them made their way through the loud, smoke-filled room, staying together as they aimed for a place at the bar in the hopes they would be able to see more faces from that vantage point. It was a standing-room-only crowd, men and rough-looking women, many of them wearing leather and chains and patches on their jackets, claiming they were outlaws.

"What gives?" Rafe asked the bartender, flashing a smile in her direction and turning on the charm, the wolf in Syndelle growling at the sight of it.

"Mud-wrestling. Thousand-dollar pot tonight." A yell went up and the bartender nodded in the direction of the crowd just as it parted to allow a dark-haired woman with bare, watermelon-sized breasts and a black G-string to wade through and climb into a ring constructed of plywood. "That's Geila, she belongs to a biker club called the Outlaw Dogs." Another roar went up. This time a gaunt redhead with bruises on her arms and torso moved through the crowd. "That's Tanya. She's a regular. Turns tricks in the back room here when her old man kicks her out of the house."

A patron at the other end of the bar slammed his beer bottle against the counter and the bartender moved to get him another one. Excitement rippled through the crowd, along with the flash of money, the gap closing so that Syndelle and the others couldn't see the fight in the muddy arena.

As the action taking place inside the ring grew more intense, it spread across the room, ratcheting up the potential for violence so that it crawled across Syndelle's skin in warning. She gave an involuntary jerk at the feel of a hand around her arm, then an embarrassed laugh when she realized just as quickly that it was Skye's. "Look at that guy over there, the one with the black-eye who's standing next to the hooker with the tassels and the screaming-red lips," Skye said. "He looks like one of the guys who came into The Hole. But I didn't get close enough to him so I'd recognize him by smell."

Syndelle studied the man and the wolf snarled in recognition. "He's one of them," she said, checking along the link with Rafael to ensure that he'd seen the man also.

Rafe nodded. "I recognize him. I saw him take a punch to the face last night."

Skye shifted away from the bar, grinning. "I think we need to get better acquainted with him."

Stay back, Brann ordered as Syndelle followed her sister. *Let Rafael and Skye deal with this.*

I will not do anything foolish.

Your being there at all is foolish, as is your leaving the compound, he said, making no effort to blunt the sting of his disapproval.

I will not be held prisoner in my own home.

He pulled back, refraining from comment, though she felt his determination to control her, she sensed his belief that once she accepted the companion bond, he would command her.

He will not, she said, a pledge to herself.

He will not, the wolf echoed. A promise for both of them.

A fight broke out behind Syndelle, a crash of glass and a slap of flesh against flesh. The wolf tensed, its sense of smell picking out the presence of guns underneath the sweat and alcohol and drugs. Rafe's hand grabbed Syndelle's wrist, propelling her forward, so that his back protected hers.

Her heart melted at the gesture, though her stomach tightened at the thought of him being hurt. There was a flash of silver in Skye's right hand, a punch by her left, followed by a slurred "Bitch!" as a drunk reeled backward into a crowd of men.

The commotion caused their prey to spot them. Recognition flashed in his eyes, along with disbelief and confusion. Syndelle braced herself for his lunge, but rather than attack, he retreated, quickly leaving the bar with them in pursuit.

It was Rafe who got to him first. Almost immediately, another man in leather and chains emerged from the bar, but before he could aid his friend, Skye attacked, knocking him to the ground and pressing the blade of her knife against his throat a second before she trapped him in her eyes.

Rafael grunted, rolling and twisting with the first man, their breaths coming in heaving pants even after Rafael had successfully pinned his prey, using a length of chain to bind the man's wrists. Syndelle knelt down next to them, capturing the man and his violent thoughts.

Only to find that his mind did not contain the information they were seeking.

Nearby Skye echoed what Syndelle had found, saying, "There's nothing here. I can see his memories of walking into the bar and noticing Syndelle and me. I can see him starting the fight then escaping afterward. But it's like the idea to do it popped into his head out of nowhere. There's no motivation, no planning. No bragging or thoughts of it afterward. It almost feels like a dream."

Vampire, Rafe growled in Syndelle's mind.

A vampire's touch, Syndelle agreed, sharing the thought with her sister as she moved to kneel next to Skye. *Whoever is behind the attack thinks to protect themselves by disappearing from human memory. But the truth of what both these men know is in their blood, and there is no hiding from that truth. Cut him, Skye, let his memories flow to me.*

Skye gasped as Gian commanded her hand to freeze, using compulsion unlike any he'd ever tried on her before, Brann's voice and power roaring down the vampire blood-link she shared with her mate and with Syndelle. *I forbid it! You will not take what he is into yourself, Syndelle! I will not allow it!*

Syndelle stiffened her spine. *There is too much at stake to pass up this chance to find out what is going on and who is behind it, Brann. Do you truly believe that all the memories that are held inside me are benign images of flowers and babies? Do not force me to challenge you directly on this matter.*

Brann hissed, a flash of sharp fangs, as compulsion and fury surged down the shared link. But Syndelle's determination won out and he retreated with a dark warning. *Do not think you can act without consequence, Syndelle. Do not think that I will let you continue to defy me once you have become my companion.*

The wolf's lips pulled back in a show of its own teeth. Its thoughts echoing words it had taken from both Skye and Rafael's memories. *We are not a pet to speak only when spoken to and behave only as ordered to behave.*

Skye snickered and Syndelle's fingers gracefully traced a series of wards before she once again said, "Cut him."

When it was done, Syndelle leaned forward, touching her lips to the stream of blood flowing from the man's neck, the truth moving unstopped, unedited into the dark abyss, his life insignificant in a vastness that encompassed everything. His life meaningless, but no less horrifying to Syndelle.

She allowed herself a moment before kneeling next to Rafael. Gian's will combining with Skye's hypnotic ability so that the man her sister had subdued remained still even after Skye had moved to the second man, cutting him as she'd done the first, freeing his memories as well.

This time when Syndelle stood, she said, "Yvonne and the human that Rafe saw with the vampire slave Frankie paid a visit to these men and their friends, offering a payment of drugs if they could take me alive, or kill me. The vampire touched their minds through Yvonne as the slave brought them to orgasm—the power behind the compulsion wasn't strong, but it wouldn't need to be given the drugs and alcohol in their systems."

"Then I guess it's a good thing we were already planning to pay another visit to Yvonne," Skye said.

Rafe's smile was fierce. "And vampire law is in our favor. At sunset Brann can compel her to leave her room and answer for her actions." He looked down at the two men. "Better call Augustino and have these two put on ice. I'm sure Syndelle can come up with a crime or two that they've committed."

They stayed only long enough for a patrol car to pick up the two men—men whose faces appeared on a number of wanted posters.

* * * * *

Skye knew as soon as they entered the hallway leading to Yvonne's room that the girl was probably dead. "Smell that?"

"Piss, vomit, and shit?" Rafe said. "I'm trying my best not to."

Skye sent him a look. "There's something dead in here."

"Got to love those wolfie senses."

Skye shook her head and looked at Syndelle. "How do you and Brann put up with him?"

"He has his talents." A small smile played over Syndelle's lips, though Skye saw a growing sadness in her sister's eyes as they neared Yvonne's door and the scent of death grew stronger.

"You should call Detective Augustino again," Syndelle said when they stopped outside of Yvonne's room.

Rafe's hand settled on the back of Syndelle's neck. "She's dead?"

"Yes."

Skye let the wolf dominate, its sense of smell well-developed and accurate. Blood. There was a lot of blood on the other side of the door. Yvonne's scent. Yvonne's blood. The taint of her master's magic washed away by her death. "If we call the cops, will it be safe for them to enter?"

Syndelle knelt down, her hand reaching out, only to be halted by Rafe's fingers around her wrist. "No foolish chances, remember?"

"There's nothing of the vampire here. Look."

Where the vampire's slave mark had been, now there was only a deeply burned place on the door.

"Shit," Rafe said, standing and pulling Syndelle to her feet as Skye brought out her cellular phone and called the police.

They retreated from the building, waiting next to Rafe's Boxster and Skye's Harley. Staying there even after Augustino had arrived with other policemen and the door to Yvonne's room was forced open.

"Looks like suicide," Augustino said a short time later. "She slit her wrists." His eyes studied Syndelle warily, but with all the humans around, he didn't speak about what happened at The Hole.

"You noticed the burn mark at the base of the door?" Rafe asked, glad he'd brought Augustino up to date on their visit to Yvonne's room when they'd met up to do the tattoo.

Augustino nodded slightly.

"What about the telescope?" Skye asked. "Was it pointed at Bangers?"

"Yes."

Rafe frowned. "Makes you wonder what other places might be watched."

Skye stiffened. "Like Fangs?"

"That would seem reasonable given all that's happened."

"Are we free to go?" Skye asked Augustino.

"Yes." His attention shifted to Rafael. "I'll see you tonight?"

"Later than usual. I need to be home at sunset. I'll call you when I'm ready to leave the house."

Augustino nodded, then turned to watch as Yvonne's shrouded body was wheeled out on a stretcher and loaded into a coroner's van.

Cleaning house, Gian whispered in Skye's mind. *The vampire is making sure that no trail leads back to him...or her. But it will do no good. Brann will not let the attack on Syndelle go unpunished.*

Nor will the Coronado Angelini. Syndelle said that they would come here before they returned to their compound.

Gian's amused pride stroked Skye like a warm caress. *If my mate is an example of what the Coronado line produces, then I almost pity anyone who is found guilty of ordering Syndelle's kidnapping or death.*

A tight knot formed in Skye's chest. Her desire to share her fears with Gian conflicting with the need to keep Syndelle's secret safe. *He will learn soon enough,* the wolf whispered in her mind, offering what comfort it could and Skye turned her thoughts back to the dead girl. *Yvonne killed herself because her vampire master denied her blood?*

Perhaps. Or perhaps the vampire tricked her, making her think that ridding herself of her human blood would enable her to rise as a vampire.

Why doesn't your council ban the making of slaves?

Because there are always those willing to sell their souls in exchange for a vampire's deadly kiss. She felt his shrug. *Once we were human, Skye, some more honorable than others, but the long centuries often strip us of our humanity. That's why our laws are rigid and detailed, because sometimes they are the only thing that keep us from becoming soulless monsters. It is better for those who desire mindless slaves to make them from the willing rather than force such a life on one who wouldn't choose it.*

I don't like it.

Nor do I. It is one of the things that has always set Brann's line apart. Speaking of which, my sire grows impatient to have his mate safely home.

Skye looked at the sun and frowned, saying to the others, "If we're going to check out the area around Fangs, we'd better get going."

"Try not to find any more bodies," Detective Augustino murmured.

It was a request they didn't honor.

Chapter Eighteen

❧

"It's the guy who was with Frankie," Rafael said as he peered into the dumpster behind Fangs, staring at the body that had been tossed inside.

They'd scoured the area around the nightclub, looking for a place that a vampire's minion could be positioned in order to see who came and went. They'd found no mark, had found nothing until Syndelle's nose had led them to the dumpster.

"Cause of death?" Skye asked.

"You've been mated to a cop too long," Rafe teased.

Skye shook her head. "A cop who's going to be very unhappy when he finds out that I've been at the scene twice today when a body was discovered. Can you tell how he was killed?"

"No." Rafe jumped down from his perch and Skye took his place.

"Not a lot of excess blood." She wrinkled her nose. "But plenty of semen. He smells like he's covered in it."

Rafe remembered the man licking a stud-pierced tongue over his lips when he'd told him to back off, how he'd challenged Rafe, saying, "Or what? Your daddy will come beat me up? I'd like that. Does he give good pain?" It made Rafe's stomach roil just thinking about it, just imagining the man's final hours. He didn't doubt that he'd gotten what he thought he wanted—pain. "Let's get out of here. Let one of Gian's people call this in."

"There's the small matter of our fingerprints," Skye pointed out.

"Wipe them."

Skye hesitated for only a second then shook her head. "No. You take Syndelle home, she didn't touch anything. I'll go inside and call Augustino one more time." She grimaced. "He's going to start dreading my phone calls."

"You do this for your human mate?" Syndelle guessed.

Skye scowled, clearly unhappy about having to follow a set of rules she didn't agree with. "Yeah. Don't ever let anyone tell you that dealing with mates is easy."

Syndelle's heart leaped and jerked in her chest as her mind brushed against Brann's, finding that his rage had firmed into implacable resolve. But she laughed and hugged her sister, saying, "Trust me, I already see how difficult having mates can be," and then she and Rafe returned home, to Brann, who prowled through their house like a hungry, dangerous tiger, his words an attack as soon as they walked through the front door.

"You will not continue to defy me, Syndelle," he said, pressing her against the wall in a show of physical strength and dominance. "I will not let you risk yourself."

Lust flashed through her, the wolf enjoying this display by its mate, despite Syndelle's irritation. "No harm has come to me and I have returned as I promised I would."

Brann's nostrils flared, the scent of her filling his body with heat. The call of her blood and Rafael's arousal a distraction he was almost unable to fight. His cock was hard, aching. His gums tingled with the need to bite. And the feel of her power brushing against his roared through him, filling him with the primitive need to conquer in a physical show of force.

"I have lived in times when men took rods to their disobedient wives," he growled, his fingernails extending to deadly talons.

"And I have not," Syndelle said, challenge in her eyes. Her gaze unflinching as Brann pressed sharp nails against her jugular vein.

Rafe moved then, lounging insolently against the wall next to them, his tone mocking when he said, "It might amuse you to try and fuck with her mind, Brann, but I would prefer to fuck other parts of her before I have to leave again."

For a long moment the air grew heavy, charged with Brann's power, the feel of it rippling around them like the buildup before a lightning strike. Syndelle and Rafe braced themselves, both watching as Brann's pupils flared, his eyes filling with a vampire's ice-blue fire, becoming alien, predatory, a promise of death—until he fought his impulses and stepped back, hissing, "Strip, Syndelle."

The wolf's smile echoed Syndelle's. This victory she could give her mate. She lowered her eyelashes as her fingers moved to the front of her shirt, slowly working down the row of buttons until the shirt spread open, exposing breasts that she hadn't bothered to contain within a bra.

She licked her lips, savoring the way Brann's face went tight, savoring the heady scent of male arousal, the sounds of rapidly beating hearts and quick breaths of air. Her fingers went to her nipples, fondling and tugging on them.

"Fuck," Rafe growled, kneeling in front of her, his hands making quick work of getting her out of her jeans and shoes, his face going instantly to the juncture between her thighs.

Syndelle cried out, using the wall behind her to brace herself against the onslaught of Rafael's mouth, her clit pulsing with its own demand even as her channel clenched, trying to capture his tongue.

Brann moved in, trapping Rafe between their bodies, one hand dropping to stroke his male companion, while the other hand captured Syndelle's face, holding it still as his lips covered hers, as his tongue thrust into her mouth in the same rhythm as Rafe's tongue pressed into her pussy.

There was no denying her need, no denying theirs. Syndelle gave herself up to them, letting them drive her higher and higher, then whimpering and begging when they pulled back just short of bringing her to orgasm.

She could feel the swirl of an unspoken conversation going on between her two mates, but the pleasure they were bringing her was so intense that she couldn't concentrate on what they were saying, she could only writhe against them, reveling in their shared desire, reveling in the promise that this was just the beginning of what they would share this night.

She sobbed when Brann stepped away. And when Rafe's mouth left her desperately hungry pussy, she speared her fingers through his hair and tried to force him back to her swollen, dripping cunt lips and engorged clitoris. He laughed, a husky sound of masculine satisfaction and yielded to her demands for a moment, swirling his tongue over and around her swollen knob as Brann opened his own shirt and dropped it to the floor before retrieving a necklace from his back pocket.

Syndelle's heart jerked at the sight of it—a chain of onyx with each link bearing a symbol, both a warning and a claim, while a coin identical to the one Rafael wore hung in the middle, suspended by woven silver strands. When Brann once again closed the gap between them, her heart filled with pleasure at the knowledge that he intended to include Rafael in this most sacred act between a vampire and the one he had chosen as a companion.

"Do you accept my offer and freely choose to become my companion, Syndelle?"

"Yes."

"Then bind your life to mine by taking my blood and wearing the medallion that shows all that you belong to me."

He leaned in, brushing his lips against hers before fastening the snug, collar-like necklace around her throat. Then he opened a gash above his heart, a moan of exquisite pleasure escaping from him at the dual sensation of Rafe's renewed assault on Syndelle's cunt and the feel of her mouth on his skin. She drew his blood deeply into her body, so deeply that it flowed into every cell and claimed her on every level, giving him power over her for all eternity, Syndelle's shuddering release sealing their companion bond.

She lay limp and sated in Brann's arms as he quickly carried her to his bedroom, Rafe's needs echoing his own so that there was no need for conversation. He paused only long enough to remove a bottle of lubricant from a drawer and hand it to Rafael before stripping out of the rest of his clothing and lying on the bed, pulling Syndelle on top of him and urging her legs apart so that his cock speared into her wet depths.

Her eyes opened and Brann's cock jerked, his heart swelling with fulfillment at the look on her beautiful face, the love and acceptance, the absolute hunger for her mates. When the walls of her channel clamped on his cock, he groaned, arching into her wet pussy, anxious for the moment when the three of them would be joined, when Rafe's penis would slide against his.

Brann's hands smoothed over her buttocks, spreading them as Rafael moved into position above them. Anticipation whipped through Syndelle and she sought Brann's mouth, welcoming his coaxing tongue, welcoming the reassuring feel of his strong body beneath hers.

Her sheath tightened even further on Brann, her vulva grew fuller, and her clit pulsed as Rafe coated her back entrance with lubricant, using first his fingers and then his arousal-wet penis, taking his time to gently open her though he shook with desire, with the desperate need to be inside her, to bathe in the all-encompassing bond between the three of them and feel Brann's cock against his as they were both held deep in Syndelle's body.

Emotion washed through Rafe. Love so profound that he knew he *would* choose death rather than to ever be without this.

Then it is good you won't have to make such a choice, Brann purred, his voice a soft stroke that had Rafe clenching his buttocks and fighting against the need to force his cock into Syndelle's virgin entrance.

Virgin. There were no words to express the depth of his feelings, other than the wash of gratitude and swelling of love that he allowed Brann to feel.

Brann had known what this gift would mean to Rafael. To be the first to have Syndelle in all the ways a man could penetrate a woman. Her cunt. Her mouth. And now her ass.

He groaned, pressing his lips to her shoulder, sucking in the springtime scent of her with each pant, tasting her desire with each wet kiss, the touch of his mouth on her skin triggering the wolf's submission, making her body go lax so that it was easier for him to enter her, until finally he was all the way in. His length separated from Brann's by only a thin barrier.

Brann's hands moved from Syndelle's buttocks, going to Rafael's hips, his sides, his ass. And the feel of a masculine touch combined with the soft whimpering sounds Syndelle was making eroded the last of Rafael's control.

Pleasure like none she could have imagined burned through Syndelle as her mates began thrusting—their hands and mouths everywhere, their bodies all that she would ever need.

As their pace quickened, she screamed and scratched and bit, fighting like a wild thing—not to escape, but to get closer to them—to yield everything that she was to them. And they took and took and took, just as they gave her all that they were. The love and lust a fire so hot, so intense that it consumed them, destroying anything that would separate them, leaving them like a phoenix rising out of the ashes of their pasts in order to embrace a future where they were one. Forever joined by Angelini magic and vampire bonds.

With a final cry, Syndelle locked Brann's cock inside her, the feel of her tight muscles holding him bringing the three of them to the precipice and shoving them over, triggering a continuous string of orgasms, ripping wave after wave of pleasure from their very souls until they were left breathless, sated, their sweat-slick bodies melded together by more than just desire.

"You are beautiful," Brann whispered, "inside and out. A priceless treasure that I will never misuse. A gift that I will always appreciate. Love is a pale, shallow word, one that can't begin to hold what you mean to me within it, Syndelle."

"Or to me," Rafe said, and Syndelle's heart swelled with not only her own emotion, but theirs as well so that she touched them with her thoughts, trying to convey without words the depth of her feelings for them both.

They made love again. Their bodies a choir singing a song of ecstasy. The melody softer, gentler the second time, but just as overpowering. The climax equally sublime.

"I've got to meet up with Augustino," Rafe said a little while later, pulling away and rising from the bed, shaking his head "no" and laughing when Brann grumbled and Syndelle stirred. "You two stay here." He leaned down, pressing a kiss to Syndelle's lips, then Brann's. "Enjoy the rest of the night. Somehow I think between Skye, Gian, Rico, and Augustino, I'll be well-guarded." He laughed, feeling lighthearted. "But don't expect me to tune in to this channel while I'm hitting the club scene. I don't intend to walk around all night with a wet stain on my crotch."

Syndelle laughed, rolling to her back so that she could look at her mate. Her heart thundering in her chest at his beauty, at the openness of his heart and soul.

Rafe shook his head, returning to the bed, lying next to her, his mouth pressing affectionate kisses along her neck, over her chin, against her lips, his nose finally rubbing against hers as he stared into her eyes. "If you don't stop looking at me like that, I'm never going to be able to leave you. I need to go—just in case we get lucky and find Justin's killer—but I don't want to relive last night, Syndelle. I don't want to worry about someone trying to kill you. I want to know that you're here, making love with Brann and enjoying the night."

Worry moved through Syndelle, along with such a mix of other emotions that her heart felt full, her chest tight. But she stayed while he left, accepting the shallow barrier he erected in order to concentrate on what he was doing away from them, wishing for the sun to rise almost as much as she wished that the night would never end. The clouds of foreboding gathering inside her, settling along the dawn in a dark omen.

Chapter Nineteen

℘

By the time the sun was just about to rise on the horizon, Rafael had decided that they needed a better plan if they were going to catch the man they were after. He'd been pinched, groped, hit on, rubbed against, and propositioned by too many men—all while he'd desperately tried to avoid knowing what Brann and Syndelle were doing. He wasn't sure that he could endure too many more nights of trolling like this. He wasn't sure how much longer Gian was going to tolerate it either.

That thought brought a small spike of pleasure to Rafe. It had been amusing to see Gian's temper grow shorter as the night faded and his chance to fuck his mate disappeared with it, until finally he was snarling as the sunrise forced him to retreat, leaving Skye and Rico together—knowing that they'd probably fuck the day away without him.

"Had enough of this fun?" Rico asked, moving to stand next to Rafe, his body close enough to give the impression that he might be trying to lure Rafe into a threesome.

"Yeah, more than enough." Rafe put an arm around Rico's shoulders, enjoying Skye's scowl when her mate tensed, still not completely comfortable with another man's touch—especially one who also loved men.

Rico frowned, mumbling "shit" before reaching for the cell phone at his waist, and Rafael guessed it was Augustino when Rico said, "I'll tell him. We're about ready to pack it in here," before hanging up and saying, "Augustino says there's a guy asking around about you at Stingers. He says the guy's sending his creep meter off the scale."

Rafe grinned. "Then it sounds like I need to make an appearance. You and Skye go ahead of me and get into position."

Rico hesitated, then shrugged. "Okay, let's wrap this up. If it's just your run-of-the-mill creep, attracted to your dubious charms, then we'll cut him loose and quit." He shook his head. "¡Carajo! This is like a fucking demotion."

Rafe stifled a laugh. Mated to a cop. He almost felt sorry for Skye.

He gave them a five-minute head start before leaving the bar, deciding to walk rather than retrace his steps and collect the Boxster. It'd be easy enough for Augustino to "pick him up" and then drop him at the car later.

Fuck, he was tired. As he moved into the dawn light, he let his mind seek Syndelle's and Brann's.

Like Gian, Brann had retreated to his daytime resting place. His presence not as solid as it was in the night, though he was still linked to Rafe, Brann's ancient power enabling him to resist the sun's command that he disappear completely. *You are on your way home?* Brann asked, and Rafe smiled at the satisfaction he could feel in Brann, at the knowledge that the hours he'd spent with their Angelini mate had left Brann sated and relaxed.

One quick stop, then I'm heading to the house.

Good. Syndelle is anxious for your return.

Rafe turned his thoughts to his mate, his wife—something he'd never dreamed of for himself. She was asleep, twisting and turning, worry for him filling her thoughts.

I'll be home soon, he said, trying to soothe her, but she seemed to grow more agitated, coming awake with a gasp just as he became aware of the footsteps behind him, the sudden presence sending his own heart thundering, making him turn and allowing him to see Frankie's face an instant before the pipe he was wielding crashed into Rafe's skull.

For a second there was a horrifying, nauseating sensation of the link being severed, but then it hummed back into place and

Syndelle staggered to her feet, grateful that Rafael was still alive—at least for the moment.

She dialed Skye's cell phone, not wanting to rely on the new bond she had with her sister in order to communicate as she directed Skye to the alley, though in her heart, Syndelle knew that it would be too late by the time her sister and the others got there.

Brann's rage swamped her, his fury, a sudden lightning bolt traveling down the line connecting him to Rafe and in the instant it struck, she saw Frankie's death, his hand locked around the coin as he ripped it from Rafael's neck.

Too late. It was too late to take back Brann's death sentence so that Frankie could be questioned. Too late to get to Rafe. Already she could feel him moving further away from her.

* * * * *

"¡Carajo! Another body!" Rico cursed, his anger directed at something he could focus on rather than the fear for Rafael that filled his gut, pouring in along with his mate's anguish and the guilt for having failed to keep Rafe safe.

"Vampire slave," Augustino hissed.

Skye nodded. "I recognize him from a memory of Rafael's that Syndelle shared with me." She looked around to make sure that they were truly alone in the alleyway. "We can't leave the necklace in his hand."

Augustino knelt down to study the corpse. "Do you trust the vampires so much that you're willing to try and remove it? Most likely it's the cause of death here, though I'm sure the coroner will rule it a heart attack."

Skye reached for Frankie's hand. "Brann won't use his power against us."

Rico grabbed her wrist. "I'll do it."

She smiled despite the horror of the situation. It was always a balancing act with both of her mates, they would try to control and protect her if she let them.

Gian's anger swirled along the link she shared with him, but he too found humor in the situation. *Let Rico show you how big his balls are since he can no longer take you back to the house and do so. No harm will come to him.*

Skye relaxed her arm, a silent signal for Rico to proceed, and within seconds he'd pried the coin from Frankie's fingers and handed it her. "Someone must have made us, they used our search for the killer to trap Rafael."

Augustino nodded. "So it would seem."

* * * * *

Fear and pain poured into Syndelle, countered quickly by the swelling of ancient power, the whispered promise that if she freed it, if she let it return, then it would aid her in the rescue of her mate. Blood called to blood, it reminded her, and Brann's presence now would make the link with Rafael a shout instead of a faint whisper.

The day was here, burning bright, the hours until sunset stretching out like a dark nightmare for all of them—especially Rafael. The killer he'd been seeking had him now, his torture and eventual death aided by vampire enemies—though hard to prove since he'd been hunting this human just as this human had been hunting him.

Perhaps the wolf and the Angelini magic could lead her to Rafe. Perhaps.

Could she really afford to take the chance that they would be enough? Could she really afford to wait?

She was Angelini, the ancient long-present voice whispered, created for a purpose and now she stood in the moment of decision. If she chose to act, there would be no going back, no hiding what she was.

She was *The Masada*.

The voice had made it so. The dark, silent abyss where the ancient vampire creation magic had been banished had claimed her long ago.

And she had proved her worth. Escaping it, navigating it, containing it. Now did she have the courage to embrace it fully, to step into her destiny?

There was no hesitation in Syndelle as her mind reached for Brann's, as her footsteps led her to his daytime resting place, her fingers undoing the ancient, impenetrable wards, guided by his trust, his knowledge, his belief that she would never harm him as he lay completely helpless.

And then she was inside the most private sanctuary in his home, just as she'd once stood in Sabin's sanctuary, guided there by her mother after the rogue werewolves had attacked.

The myth claimed that a blood sacrifice was needed. And it was so, though the magic had to be willing to flow from one vessel into another.

It had been willing that day she'd stood next to her father's still form. The day she'd bitten down hard, blooding her own lips before bending over to press her mouth to his in a chaste kiss — in a gift that had remained a more closely guarded secret than her existence.

She leaned over and pressed her mouth to Brann's, her blood and magic seeping into him, calling him fully to his body, bringing him into the daylight.

His chest heaved and his heart thundered to life. His eyes opened and his arms wrapped around Syndelle, pulling her down on top of him before rolling to cover her body with his.

Hunger and triumph roared through him, momentarily suppressing the rage and fear at Rafael's abduction, leaving nothing in its wake but the need to couple with Syndelle. He turned her kiss of life into one of love and lust, insatiable desire and physical worship, and she writhed underneath him, the ancient power yielding to the wolf's claim and the Angelini magic, the scent of her arousal swamping Brann's senses, overwhelming him, so that he took her forcefully, plunging in and out of her body like an animal in a frenzied, rough mating.

His cock demanding that she lock him to her as he sucked the blood from her lips.

Only after the incredible hunger was sated was Brann able to rise from his resting place, heart racing in his chest, the rush of his own blood a roar in his mind as he dressed, anxious now to move into the day. "Ready to hunt?" he asked, taking Syndelle's hand.

Syndelle's eyes met his.

Sorcerer. Executioner. Vampire.

He'd once been the mate of her nightmares. The bogeyman she'd feared. But now they stood as equals.

"I'm ready."

Chapter Twenty

ॐ

Pain ripped through Rafe's head. He couldn't move and for a second he wasn't too worried about it. Then terror tried to force its way in, coming with the memory of Frankie in the alley.

Rafe forced himself to lie still, to keep his eyes closed, to reach for Syndelle and Brann before panic set in. His heart jerked, a wild beat in his ears, when his mind struck a barrier. A chilly sweat covered his body, a shiver rushed all the way to his soul, opening the doorway and allowing fear to wash over him.

Memories of his childhood threatened to swamp him. The times he'd had to lie still, to pretend he didn't know what was happening around him. He squelched them, cursing Diego, promising himself that one day he would be successful in hunting the cult leader down and sending him to hell—sending his followers along with him.

Fuck. No time for that now.

Rafe cursed himself for not paying attention, for not even guessing that he was walking into a trap. He was smarter than that. *Like Justin had been.*

Rafe shoved images of Justin's corpse aside, forcing himself to concentrate on his own situation. He was naked. Ankles taped together. Arms, too, but behind his back. Concrete floor underneath him. Cold and rough against his cheek and chest. His cock limp for the first time since he'd seen Syndelle walk into Bangers.

Syndelle. His mind reached again, a fist squeezing around his heart, painful and ruthless. He ached for her. For them.

He felt the absence of the companion necklace then and his stomach tightened. Was that why he couldn't touch Brann's mind? Because he'd run scared for the last two years? Giving Brann blood—when forced—but never again taking it from Brann as he had that night at Drac's, never reinforcing the link.

I know you'll fight me, Rafael, even if you save yourself by becoming my companion. So I'll tell you now, deny my claim to you afterward if you must and for as long as you choose.

What a fucking waste of time that had been. If he could do it over again…

At least he could have learned some of what Brann knew, some of what Brann had offered to teach him.

He could think of any number of wards and chants that would have come in handy now. Rafe's thoughts stilled at the sound of footsteps. It took all his willpower not to open his eyes, not to fight and struggle when a tennis shoe landed against his ribs, hard enough to make him jerk and moan.

"Wake up!" a man's voice demanded in the second before another kick landed on Rafe's ribs, this one hard enough to send pain shooting through his side in a sharp, hard jolt.

He didn't give in to the demand even when his ribs and back got the full impact of an angry stomp. Tears formed at the corners of his eyes, but remained hidden by his hair. Fuck. He hurt.

His attacker moved away and Rafe risked a glance. All he could see at first was blue jeans and tennis shoes on a pudgy figure. Dated shirt and a short haircut, a basement room that was windowless, unfinished.

The man disappeared through a doorway and there was the sound of water pounding hard against plastic. Rafe lifted his head, checking for ways out. Seeing only the door the man had gone through.

The water stopped. Rafael dropped his head but peeked through lowered lashes.

Acne-scarred face, fleshy, the pudge extended to the front. Soft and out of shape. Loser.

It radiated off the guy like stink off a carcass and Rafe's cock shriveled further as Augustino's words flashed through his mind. *Four unsolved homicides, all with the same victim profile — male, blond with long hair, inverted pentacle tattoo somewhere on the body. There's a fifth victim. No tattoo on him, but the damage done to him was identical to the other four, so I think he was killed by the same perp. All five victims were roughed up, shock burns consistent with the use of a cattle prod, sodomized — ass and mouth — with genitals removed as a final insult.*

Fucking vampire politics. Yvonne's master must have somehow found the crazy bastard who'd killed Justin and attacked Big Daddy's girls, must have recognized him — even if Yvonne didn't — or maybe her owner had enjoyed taunting her with the sight of the man who'd raped and tortured her — the man who'd left her so badly scarred that she'd traded her soul in order to get her looks back.

Shit. The attack on Syndelle made sense now. Yvonne's telescope was focused on Bangers. She'd probably seen Rafe leave with Syndelle — and if Fangs was also being watched, which seemed likely, then the vampire would have learned that Syndelle left with Brann. Could have easily guessed that Syndelle was more than an easy fuck.

Lilith. She had to be behind the attack. Someone on the council must have told her that Brann had been sent to Las Vegas to deal with a witch and the fledgling vampires the witch had managed to create. It would have taken little effort for Lilith to learn that even though the matter had been resolved, Brann was still here, as was he. Syndelle had seen Ishana in the casino, probably because Lilith had wanted to learn about the female Brann might make his companion, perhaps she'd even planned on having her companion kill Syndelle then — except they'd sensed the Angelini blood in Syndelle and known it would be foolish to openly attack her.

The thought of Brann growing more powerful through an Angelini bond would have filled Lilith with rage. She had lusted for Brann's power for centuries. But vampire marriages of the type Lilith wanted were rare, even among fledglings, and Brann's refusal even to couple with her had fueled her hate, channeling it into a thirst for revenge.

Rafe shivered as he saw the design of Lilith's elaborate, deadly trap—and realized that this was where she'd intended he would end up all along—his death untraceable to her.

Why did you send Rafe to Bangers? Syndelle had asked.

There have been a number of new slaves at Wyldfyres, faces I have seen in Rafe's memories of Bangers.

All women that he'd fucked.

She'd guessed that Brann would send Rafe. She'd known all along that Justin's killer would target him. But she hadn't counted on…

Rafe wasn't able to keep himself from screaming when cold water struck him, followed immediately by the press of a cattle prod on his ass.

The man standing over him laughed gleefully, lowering the cattle prod so that it was in front of Rafe's face as he bent down and pulled Rafael's hair out of the way. "Are we having fun, Tommy?" he said in a singsong voice that had every nerve ending on Rafe's body reacting.

"I'm not Tommy," Rafael said, already knowing it didn't matter whether he was or not.

The guy above him laughed and unzipped his pants, pulling his penis out. "Oh, that's right, I'm supposed to call you master," he said, his singsong voice and his crazy eyes making Rafe more frightened than the sight of him jerking off, masturbating with quick, impatient strokes, the cattle prod wavering in the air in front of Rafe's face until he couldn't stand it anymore and rolled away just as a stream of come hit the concrete where he'd been lying.

"No!" the guy screamed, striking out with his feet and then the cattle prod. "No! You're going to take it just like you made me take it! And then you're going to die, you cunt-whore!"

* * * * *

Syndelle gripped Brann's leg tightly, her fingers curled around his thigh as he shifted gears before covering her hand with his. "We are close. And he is alive."

"I know," she said, trying to draw comfort from the knowledge that the man who had Rafe liked to torture his victims before he killed them—though the thought of Rafael being hurt was a twisting agony in Syndelle's gut.

He can be healed, Brann said. *But I cannot bring him back from death. Nor can you. His mind is strong, he has seen worse, survived worse.* There was a fleeting image of a young Rafe dressed in a white robe with a strange blood-red symbol on it, an older man with a long beard who looked at Rafael with lust and commanded all those around him, his hand resting on a whip as he lectured his followers on pain and discipline and the cleansing of the soul—his eyes burning with an intensity that made Syndelle shy away. *Diego.* The name whispered in Syndelle's mind, borne by Rafe's blood memories, the emotion surrounding it feeding the wolf's need to savage any who would threaten its mate.

"A hunt for another day," Brann said, bringing Syndelle's hand to his mouth, the brush of his lips a gesture meant to calm as well as a promise that all would be well.

They turned into a neighborhood, a quiet place that spoke of peace and yet harbored one of dark violence. Brann slowed the Viper, crawling along until he found what they were searching for, the vampire companion bond leading him to the house that contained Rafael.

When Brann would have ordered Syndelle to stay in the car, she pushed the door open and said, "I am not so foolish as to go in first, but do not waste your breath on a command that won't be obeyed."

Despite the seriousness of the situation, Brann smiled, his heart warming with pride at the courage of his Angelini mate. The future lay ahead of them, a dangerous, twisting path that would have to be navigated carefully, but fate had smiled on him by giving him two fine companions to make the journey with.

* * * * *

Blood poured from Rafe's mouth and the breath jerked in and out of his body in painful blasts. He'd lost track of how many ribs he thought were broken. Too many. Too many, and the last kick to his head had made him black out long enough so that when he came to he found himself tied down, spread-eagle with his ass in the air like an offering—the sound of his attacker jerking off somewhere behind him competing with the race of his heart and his struggling lungs.

He screamed silently—for Brann, for Syndelle. Not believing that his life was going to end like this—not now, not when his heart had finally found a safe haven.

A pair of tennis shoes hit the floor next to Rafe's face, then a pair of jeans. He braced himself. His mind moving away from what was getting ready to happen to his body, just as it had when he'd first run from the cult, penniless, clueless, on his own and learning fast that the quickest way to earn enough money for food and a safe place to sleep was to sell himself. He concentrated on the duct tape holding his wrists to metal rings screwed into the floor. Rubbing back and forth, trying to weaken the tape so he could free his hands. If he could just free his hands...

* * * * *

Syndelle studied the symbols and wards painted in goat's blood on the doorjamb. They were primitive, knowable to humans and nonhumans alike, but effective for keeping things of a supernatural nature contained—for trapping Rafael's psychic cries inside along with anyone unwary enough to race in without caution. *Do you wish to do the honors?* Brann asked, his hand moving to touch her back, to brace her against the onslaught of Rafe's pain once the wards were down.

Her hands lifted in answer, making quick work of unraveling the trap, a small cry escaping when the way was clear and her mind touched Rafe's.

* * * * *

Relief surged through Rafe, along with an overwhelming love as Brann and Syndelle suddenly filled the bond. Tears escaped. *Anytime now would be great,* he managed to joke, feeling hot breath and clammy hands on his back.

A door crashed open in another part of the house. His attacker surged to his feet, scrambling for his clothing but finding himself slammed against the wall instead, Brann's hand locked to his throat, his eyes ripping into those of Rafe's attacker, his mind ruthlessly stripping the man of his thoughts.

Tears streamed down Syndelle's face as she used her fingers and teeth to free Rafael from the duct tape and help him sit. *I'm okay. It's okay now,* Rafe said, pressing his lips to hers, feeling her need to touch him, her reluctance to do so for fear of bringing him pain.

"He knows nothing," Brann hissed. The desire to kill rolling off him in angry waves.

"Leave him for Augustino to deal with," Syndelle said, her thoughts moving to Big Daddy. "Leave him for the humans."

Brann's fingers tightened on the man's throat for an instant before he yielded to Syndelle's request, released the man so that he slid to the floor in a whimpering heap, reduced to helplessness by Brann's command.

Cut that one a little close, Rafe joked as Brann moved to kneel next to him.

Brann's hands went to the buttons of his shirt, his fingernail extending into a talon. "Will you take what I offer, or do you intend to lurch around the house and play on Syndelle's sympathies?"

Rafe's laugh became a bloody cough. *I'll take what you offer.*

Brann opened a gash on his chest then moved closer, his arms embracing Rafael, Syndelle's hands stroking both of their backs, her face pressed to Brann's shoulder as his blood raced through Rafael, a fire burning away Rafe's injuries while he bathed in the warmth of safety and love.

Only when Rafael pulled away did he realize that his senses were telling him it was still morning. Rafe's eyes went to Syndelle. Shock moved through him, understanding, joy and fear—a mixed, wild rush of emotion that had him pulling her to him, burying his face in her hair.

Anytime you want to share the big secret about Syndelle… Fuck. He'd never guessed that *this* was it. The enormity of trying to keep her safe just about overwhelmed him.

Brann's hand stroked along his spine, the touch sending a rush of blood to Rafe's cock, making him aware of his nakedness and distracting him from his worry about Syndelle. "Guess my clothes and the coin both got ripped off."

"Skye has your companion necklace," Syndelle said.

"Skye?"

"Frankie took it."

"And died for it?"

"Yes."

"Before or after Brann found out who he belonged to?"

"His last thought was of Andre," Brann growled.

Syndelle saw an image of the vampire in Rafe's mind, but his tone was disbelieving when he said, "Andre the ass-licker?"

"Yes." Brann stood, offering a hand to both Rafe and Syndelle.

"What about him?" Rafe asked, looking at the man who'd kicked and beaten him, who'd planned on raping and then killing him. "What did he know?"

Brann's gaze also went to their prisoner. "His mind is a tangle of fantasy and reality, confusion between the present and the past. He revenges himself on a girl named Brenda—his older sister—who played at being a witch, watching and joining in, while her boyfriend Tommy sodomized him. He saw you in Bangers weeks ago and chose you then, now he thinks it was justice that a man, Frankie, offered him a chance to fuck you after he'd been asking about you at Stingers. He barely noticed Frankie in the alley, didn't even stop to see whether he was dead or alive."

"Fuck, let's get out of here," Rafe said, turning away. "Let Augustino have him. Andre is a nobody, even as a vampire. He isn't behind this. You and I both know that. If Lilith hasn't already destroyed him, then he'll spill his guts when confronted with the council's favorite executioner." Rafe shot a look at Brann. "I assume you plan to hunt him when the sun sets."

"Of course." One hand clasped Syndelle's arm, the other Rafe's. "Let us summon Augustino and then return home. Long have I dreamed of making love in the sunshine, bathed in light instead of darkness."

Chapter Twenty~One

∞

Syndelle thought that Brann would lead them to the elaborate maze of flowers and trees and ancient statues behind the house, but instead he led them to his bedroom, his lips brushing against Rafael's before moving to Syndelle's, his tongue stroking in and out of her mouth in a promise of pleasure. "I thought we'd begin in the shower," Brann said, stepping back and binding his hair, then braiding Syndelle's as Rafe did the same to his own.

The two men made short work of stripping Syndelle of her clothing, then their own, their hands petting and stroking her, making her cry out as they explored her wet folds and hidden crevices, as they teased over her clit and tugged on her nipples, their mouths on her shoulders, her neck, her ears, their bodies rubbing and pressing against hers, enticing her with the exquisite feel of skin against skin.

Lust rolled over her, the wolf's desire to feel more of its mates than just their mouths and hands. Brann and Rafe both laughed, husky sounds of male approval. *Soon*, Brann said, *soon you will feel both of our cocks at the same time.*

The wolf shivered in anticipation, Syndelle's nipples tightened and her channel spasmed, suddenly hungry to feel the lash of a strong, masculine tongue. She whimpered and Rafe dropped to his knees in front of her, his hands going to her hips, his face nuzzling her cunt, making her clit ache and pulse as his cheeks and lips rubbed against the soft down of hair between her legs, teasing her with the promise of pleasure, with the nearness of his mouth and tongue, with the heat of his breath. Brann's body pressed against her back, his hands moving around to cover her breasts, his fangs gently grazing her neck. "Do you offer to feed us both from your body, Syndelle?"

She arched in response, her body ravenous for their touch, their possession. "Yes," she pleaded, "take what you need, what you want."

Brann's tongue licked over the mark on her neck as Rafe's tongue traced her slit. Brann's lips sucked at her skin as Rafe's pulled on her swollen cunt lips.

Over and over again they alternated between licking and sucking as they held her body tightly between them, forcing her to whimper and beg, to fight against their restraint until all three of them were covered in a sheen of sweat, their chests heaving and their faces taut with the need to merge completely.

Now, Brann said, his voice a rough growl, the only warning Syndelle had before his fangs sank into her neck in the same instant that Rafe's tongue plunged into her slit, both of them feasting on her as though they were starving, their pleasure making her weak and strong at the same time, their desire and love making her heart soar as her body shook with orgasm.

Though she could have made it to the shower on her own, Syndelle enjoyed the feel of Brann's strong arms around her as he carried her there, she enjoyed the feel of his chest against her naked body, the midnight scent of him mixed with the heady smell of aroused male. His cock was full, his balls large and heavy, a predator in his prime.

And she was his mate.

The wolf licked its lips in anticipation, as did Syndelle when she turned her attention to Rafael who'd entered the large shower first and was adjusting the spray, the hot wash of it striking his chest and running down to the dark blond hair between his legs, the cock that was every bit as long as Brann's though not as thick. *Mine,* the wolf intoned. Still pleased with the first of its mates.

Ours, Syndelle said, laughing even as the wolf's desire to explore Rafe's cock with its tongue became her own need, her own craving.

Brann moved into the shower then and set her on her feet. "Perfect," Syndelle said, meaning both the temperature of the water and the two men who shared it with her.

She placed her hands on their chests, stroking a lazy path from nipple to nipple, then lower. "My turn now," she said, lashes dropping and tongue peeking provocatively between her lips.

"Only if you hurry," Brann growled, and feminine power pulsed through Syndelle at the sight of his straining cock, at the lust she saw mirrored on Rafael's face.

She went to her knees, letting her hands slip down and take possession of their penises, her thumbs teasing the engorged heads, tracing back and forth over sensitive skin and leaking slits.

"Syndelle," Brann warned.

She laughed. Full of a power she'd never imagined herself having. With a flex of her wrists, her two mates moved closer to one another, so that their cocks were almost touching, and she saw the way their buttocks clenched in anticipation, the way their bodies tightened with expectation.

She covered the head of Rafe's cock with her mouth, pleasure driving him forward so that his arms reached for Brann for support, and she rewarded him with the lash of her tongue, by suckling his cock until he was crying out. And then she did the same to Brann. Knowing without looking up that the feel of her mouth on him, the lashes she was giving Brann with her tongue were being mimicked as his lips met Rafe's, as his tongue dueled with Rafe's.

She rubbed the heads of their cocks together, driving them higher by taking them both in her mouth and tormenting them with licks and sucks, the sounds of their groans music to her ears, their lust a symphony she'd never tire of hearing.

.

Enough! Brann said, breaking away first and pulling her to her feet, the wild urge to fuck visible on his face. *Enough,* he repeated, his hand moving to grasp his own cock in a silent command for it to cease its demands.

The wolf preened at the sight, making Syndelle smile, her heart thrilling with the knowledge that this ancient, powerful vampire was hers.

Ours, the wolf said, shaking itself as though drying off, urging Syndelle to hurry up and do the same.

They moved through the bedroom, Brann stopping only long enough to retrieve the lubricant, before sliding open a hidden door and ushering them into a cozy, glass-enclosed garden where the scent of flowers and the feel of the sun's warm rays embraced them as powerful wards snapped into place to protect them. A large futon lay spread out on a wooden frame and Syndelle could easily imagine Brann lying in this private room underneath the stars and the moon as he longed for the sun's touch on his skin.

Rafe flopped on the bed, but Syndelle eluded Brann's grasp, dancing away from him as love and pleasure flooded her again at the sight of Rafael, at the knowledge that he was here with them, safe. "I want this first time out here to be a celebration of Rafael's safe return to us," she said, her voice a sultry breeze that had both men's cocks beading with moisture.

Brann laughed, a husky purr that never failed to stroke over Syndelle's body. But he complied, lying down on his side next to Rafael, his hand trailing across Rafe's chest and over his abdomen, his smile directed at Syndelle as he said, "But you will join us?"

She slid onto the bed then, coming to a rest on Rafe's opposite side, her hand teasing over his nipple and playing with the ruby-studded barbell as she leaned forward to brush a kiss over Brann's mouth, then Rafael's. "You can touch my mind and know that love doesn't begin to capture what I feel for both of you. There is no place I'd rather be than with my mates."

Her hand moved to cover Brann's, to push it lower and position it over Rafael's cock. Rafe jerked, a pant escaping as both Syndelle and Brann fondled his penis and testicles, his body arching when Syndelle leaned over to lave and suckle his nipple and Brann mirrored what she was doing. The feel of their lips making Rafe cry out as his fingers tangled in their hair.

Tears threatened to spill from his eyes. Emotion swamping him momentarily as the strength of what both Brann and Syndelle felt for him poured into his heart and soul, completely filling an aching, empty hole that he'd carried inside him since his earliest memory.

Fuck, he'd been scared—not so much of torture and death—but of losing this when he'd only just found it.

He cried out again, the pleasure of first Syndelle's tongue swirling over the head of his cock, then Brann's, chasing away thoughts of the past and the future—leaving him suspended in the moment, in a hot rush of lust and love. Over and over again their tongues and lips tormented him, their sighs and moans joining his as their fingers toyed with his balls and teased around the pucker of his anus, working lubricant into his tight hole until he was pleading for release.

With a satisfied purr, Brann moved back up Rafe's body, his lips melding with Rafael's as Syndelle latched onto the ruby-studded nipple, their touch driving Rafe's thighs further apart in silent invitation for Brann to settle on top of him. Brann groaned, accepting what was offered, trapping Rafe's cock between the two of them and nearly coming undone when Syndelle's hand wrapped around his penis and guided it to Rafe's back opening before trailing over Brann's hip and down the crevice of his own ass, the feel of her there making him surge all the way into Rafe.

Syndelle pulled away then, the dark pleasure in her eyes as she watched her two mates coupling rolling through them, compelling them as surely as if she'd given them a command. There was no holding back. No denying her or each other. There was only the rough need to fuck and fuck hard, to fuck until hot jets of semen erupted from cocks that would rise again almost immediately, cocks that would know Syndelle as thoroughly as they knew each other.

Chapter Twenty~ Two

Skye and Gian joined them outside of WyldFyres a few minutes after sunset—the sight of Gian's raised eyebrows and smirk sending a bolt of renewed irritation through Brann. Irritation that once again he'd been unable to compel Syndelle to do his bidding, to stay home where he knew she would be safe.

Despite a day of loving, of sex both carnal and tender, her will had not faltered, even when compulsion had given way to threats. *You will not leave me here while you and Rafe go there*, she'd said, determination written in every line of her body. Her fingers toying with the coin on her necklace while her eyes flashed with the silent message that she was his equal and he risked much if he confused a companion with a slave. *You have marked me as yours to protect, none would be so foolish as to probe, none will know anything beyond what is obvious, that Angelini blood flows through my veins—as does yours. Even my sister's mate doesn't know what I am and he is an ancient of your line! So do not try to scare me with dire predictions and phantom bogeymen!*

'Round and 'round they'd gone, with Rafael stretched lazily on the bed, wisely staying out of the battle, until Brann had relented, settling for a promise from Syndelle that she would stay by his side, or Gian's.

Think before you speak or I will command you to silence, Brann growled as Gian opened his mouth, no doubt to needle him with some barb about Angelini mates.

Skye rolled her eyes before glancing at Rafe, snickering, then saying, "Gian has your medallion. He fixed the chain for you, shortening it while he was at it."

Rafe laughed. "And I'm sure Brann approves. You can see what Syndelle wears. A collar. Though Brann is having a hard time finding a place to attach the leash."

Brann hissed, but amusement overwhelmed his aggravation. After centuries of being feared and pandered to, he enjoyed the sharp wit of his companion. And in truth, it pleased him that the vampires of his line were like Gian, irreverent and unafraid.

He held out his hand and Gian retrieved Rafe's companion necklace from his pocket, both of their eyes widening when his hand touched Brann's and the ancient magic stirred to life with the promise of sunshine. *You are changed?* Gian said, disbelief and hope roaring through him as his heart thundered in his chest. *Syndelle?*

Yes. She is the one we have long waited for.

Take her home then, keep her safe. I will attend to this matter on your behalf. I will question Andre and execute him when he is judged guilty.

Warmth rushed through Brann at Gian's concern for Syndelle's safety, for Gian's willingness to risk death himself should a challenge arise. Even so, he couldn't resist saying, *And you will send your Angelini mate to Fangs so that Syndelle doesn't worry for her sister as well as her sister's mate?*

Gian grimaced, daring a look at Skye whose very expression said he'd be a fool to try and send her away. "Perhaps there is safety in numbers. Shall we go in and find Andre?"

Brann laughed and turned to Rafe, placing the companion necklace on him. "Yes. I imagine the expression on Andre's face when he sees both of my companions will spare us much questioning."

Skye frowned. "How can you be so sure that he's here? How come he's not in hiding already? He must know that you'll come after him for ordering his slave to attack Rafe."

Brann shook his head. "For all his years, Andre has never gained much power. That's why he was unable to make the men who attacked Syndelle forget their actions completely. He was only able to alter their thoughts by weakening them with drugs, then touching their minds at the moment they spewed their seed into Yvonne. As for Frankie, he will know that his slave is dead, but not how or why, unless he has paid a visit to the police station or the morgue and asked. Andre would not expend such energy on beings who were disposable from the first moment he met them."

Unlike what Syndelle had seen in Rafe's memories of Drac's, WyldFyres was gaudy, a tribute to the lusts and sins to be had in Las Vegas. Male slaves guarded the doors, clad only in G-strings, though one also sported a feather boa and long, painted nails.

They stood aside, opening the doors, their gazes hastily averted when Brann stiffened at the sight of their eyes touching Syndelle and Rafe. Their whispered "Pardon, Master" holding real fear.

Gian directed a question at the more masculine of the two slaves. "How many are inside?"

"Twenty, no more than thirty, Master."

"Andre is within?"

The slave shivered. "Yes, Master."

"And Lilith?"

"Yes, Master."

Screams greeted them as soon as they stepped inside. Sounds of pain and terror that had nothing to do with what some subjected themselves to for pleasure.

The wolf stirred in Syndelle, reacting to the violence, to the scent of blood. Its body vibrating with the primitive urge to attack, to rip at flesh, the screaming a trigger urging it to join the frenzy and kill.

Brann and Gian shifted, putting themselves in front of the women while Rafe moved behind them. Syndelle's mind touched Skye's and found her also battling with the wolf of their line, subduing it with the promise that should the need arise to defend them, she would not hold it back.

"So far this is not a real sexual turn-on," Skye muttered, casting a look in Syndelle's direction. *It's not even close to what I imagined after talking with you and Rafe.*

Gian's teeth flashed white in the dim hallway. "The night is young, and for some, this is the appetizer. Each club has its own flavor, though this one varies with the diners who are in attendance."

"I think I'll pass on the meals that get served here," Rafe said, his hand stroking along Syndelle's back and she knew without probing that the scene they were about to enter bordered too closely along memories from his childhood.

When my family arrives, I will ask some of my brothers to join in the hunt for Diego and his followers. None are better at tracking than the Coronado Angelini who can take the shape of wolves.

Emotion rolled through Rafe, unchecked and unhidden, flowing into Syndelle and making her heart swell with love. *You are my life*, he said.

As is Brann, she reminded, and felt Rafael's smile along their bond.

As is Brann. When he's not being a pain in my ass.

They stepped through a doorway, stopping just inside. Vampires and their slaves and companions lounged on couches, some feeding, but most were idly watching as a thin vampire shook out the lash of his whip, his focus on the whimpering, blood-covered man whose feet were tethered to the floor while his naked body sagged, held upright, arms spread, wrists bound to a bar suspended from the ceiling.

"Is this your newest slave, Andre?" Brann asked, his voice a smooth purr. "If you're not careful, he'll be just as dead as Yvonne and Frankie."

The vampire's fear at hearing Brann's voice rippled across Syndelle's senses and the wolf licked its lips as the ancient magic stirred deep within her, judging Andre unfit without even seeing his face.

Brann motioned toward the nearly dead human. "Release him. Andre will be taking his place. By our laws, he is mine to punish as I see fit — even unto death — for the actions of his slave, Frankie, who assaulted my companion Rafael and turned him over to a man who is even now in police custody for raping, torturing, and killing other humans."

"I have done nothing to you. You can prove nothing."

Gian and Brann stepped aside, and true terror passed over Andre's features at the sight of Rafael, Syndelle, and Skye. At the sudden awareness that there were Angelini present, and even bound to vampires and without the tattoos of a hunter, none would question their word if they had evidence supporting Brann's claims.

"Do any here dispute my right to punish Andre?" Brann said, even as slaves removed the human and other vampires, afraid of Brann's wrath or perhaps wanting to enjoy a different type of entertainment, made short work of subduing Andre and placing him in the blood-coated restraints.

Lilith stood, her sultry companion rising with her, both stepping forward as though intending to leave.

Brann smiled with feral pleasure. "I think not," he said, his power pulling on Syndelle's as he chanted words so ancient that they sprung from the dark abyss within her, creating an impenetrable barrier along the border of the room, trapping everyone inside.

Murmurs of protest and excitement bounced off the unseen wall, but none dared challenge Brann directly, not even Lilith. With a thought, Brann told Gian and Rafael to stay at the edge of the circle, guarding Syndelle and Skye. Then he moved forward, picking up the dropped whip before stopping in front of Andre, whose terror now fed some of the vampires who'd only a few minutes earlier been enjoying Andre's torment of the human. "You will die, Andre. Nothing you can say will spare you that fate." Brann shook out the whip. "But I offer you the choice of how you will die. And how long it will take you to do so. Whether or not you provide a night's worth of entertainment and then meet the sun's rays, or whether you die quickly, your passing gentle when you deserve far worse." He cracked the whip, its tip a dark flicker that made Syndelle think of a snake's tongue leaving behind an ugly red mark where it caressed Andre's cheek.

"Do you admit that the human known as Frankie was your slave?" Brann asked, the lash of the whip slithering across the floor as though anxious to rear up and strike again.

"Yes."

"Was the human known as Yvonne also your slave?"

"Yes."

"And through her you ordered the attack on Syndelle?" The black lash undulated at a faster rate.

"I didn't know you had claimed her," Andre whined. "I didn't know she was Angelini."

"But you admit that you ordered the attack?"

Andre sent a desperate look toward Lilith, who'd returned to her seat and was stroking her companion's now bare breast, her eyes expressing only boredom at the events unfolding in front of her.

"I did it for Lilth," Andre said. "She wanted the woman and Rafe dead. She told me about the human killer and sent Yvonne to me."

The snakelike motion of the whip stopped and Brann moved closer, his eyes boring into Andre's. "I can easily take your thoughts, so do not bother lying to me. Did Lilith or her companion or any one of her slaves ask you to have Rafael or Syndelle killed?"

"Ishana. Ishana asked me to take Syndelle or have her killed. She told me to arrange for Rafe to fall into the killer's hands. She shared some of her blood with me and promised that Lilith would do the same if I would do this for them."

Satisfaction moved across Brann's face as he turned toward Lilith and her companion. "Do you deny Andre's claim?"

With cool grace, Ishana stood. "I freely admit that I asked Andre to strike out at Rafael's woman and Rafael. I did so without Lilith's knowledge and to settle an old grievance with Rafael. Because of his actions at Drac's two years ago, his failure to tell me that he belonged to you before fucking me, I was punished by Lilith, cast out of her bed and humiliated until she found it within her to forgive me." A triumphant smile settled on Ishana's face. "Our rules are quite clear on this. When an insult that would warrant a death penalty is brought about because of a grievance between companions, then it is the companions who must settle it—fighting to the death or until the one who claims them concedes defeat and yields a boon of the victor's choosing."

Syndelle tensed, Brann's instant uneasiness colliding with Rafe's surge of joy. Ishana turned to the others in the room. "Do all agree that those are our rules?"

A murmur signified the truth of the law and Ishana turned back around, her gaze falling on Syndelle, her lips curling in expectation. "Since my first act warranting punishment under our laws was to arrange for an attack against the Angelini female who is now Brann's companion, then it is my right to fight her first."

Lilith stood then, her eyes flicking dismissively at Andre. Her smile pure evil. "Dispose of him, Brann. He has served his purpose."

Hatred blasted through Brann. A desire to violate the law and destroy Lilith and Ishana where they stood—but to do so was to sentence Syndelle and Rafael to a living hell. He moved in to a struggling Andre, and with ancient words he traced a symbol on the other vampire's forehead, then watched impassively as the life force animating him flickered out and his organs dissolved, his skin shrinking and folding in, drying so that within seconds he looked like the mummified remains pulled from an ancient tomb.

When Brann turned back toward Lilith, he found that she'd already drawn a combat circle. Another vampire stood in its center, holding a velvet-lined case containing the athames used in such challenges.

Ishana had stripped off her clothing and waited next to Lilith. "You can concede now, Brann, and spare your unmarked Angelini this disgrace," Lilith purred.

Despair and anger swamped Brann, along with fear and self-loathing. Why had he not seen this trap? Why had he not found a way to destroy Lilith in all the centuries that they'd battled? To risk Syndelle this way...and yet to grant Lilith a boon...

Do you have so little faith in your Angelini mate? Syndelle teased, her rapidly pounding heart making the calmness of her voice a lie.

Syndelle...

Rafe pulled her to him, blaming himself for this moment, for not leaving Drac's, for...

Enough! the wolf growled. *We are not defenseless!*

"Do you grant a boon, Brann? Or does your companion answer the challenge?" Lilith asked.

Syndelle answered for him by pulling away from Rafe and stripping, her arms covering with goose bumps as she felt the eyes of so many strangers moving over her body, as the wolf's hackles rose. Without a word she entered the circle, watching as Ishana confidently did the same.

Both of them stopped within reach of the athames. The vampire holding them directed his attention to Syndelle. "Since you are the one accepting the challenge, you may choose the first blade."

She nodded though her fingertips tingled as her talons grew ready to emerge. Her mind raced, crowded with her mother's warnings and teachings. To handle a knife and draw blood with it while there was so much magic was to risk turning it into an object of power. But to refuse was to give up an advantage of surprise. Syndelle took the knife in her right hand, her weak hand.

The vampire offered the remaining athame to Ishana, then said, "In accordance with our laws, neither Brann nor Lilith can use their power to interfere, nor can you draw upon their power. The circle has been warded so that to do either is to be marked as defeated. The challenge begins as soon as I step outside the circle of challenge. You will fight to the death unless either Brann or Lilith calls a halt." He closed the empty box and moved away. As he did so, Syndelle and Ishana began circling each other, studying each other.

Wait, the wolf whispered, growing larger inside Syndelle, filling her more fully than it had ever done. Its instincts dominating. Its thoughts guiding Syndelle's movements.

They circled for endless minutes, Syndelle only barely aware of Ishana's mouth moving, of her taunting words, of the hatred and determination that burned in the other woman's eyes. The wolf wasn't interested in those things. It cared only about what Ishana's body was saying. It cared only about watching…waiting, then jumping out of reach as Ishana lunged, the deadly blade missing Syndelle by a wide margin, Ishana's hiss of fury satisfying to the wolf.

They resumed. 'Round and 'round.

The wolf was a patient hunter. It could play this game all day. But it would prefer to kill this threat and return home with its mates.

Filth spewed from Ishana's lips after a second, then a third miss.

Anticipation rippled through the wolf. *Get ready*, it whispered, shrinking inside Syndelle, yielding control. *Now!*

Syndelle dropped the athame. Trusting the wolf without question.

Pain whipped through her fingers, the poison-filled talons emerging just as Ishana attacked. Syndelle swung, raking across Ishana's chest even as the wolf danced away from the flashing knife, moving to the edge of the circle and stopping, separated from its mates and allies by only the thin line.

Fury filled Ishana's face, then agony as she fell to the floor, screaming and writhing, her body thrashing in a death that filled the room with fear.

Lilith screamed. A sound of rage and grief as she hurtled herself into the circle, grabbing the discarded knife and rushed toward Syndelle, attacking—only to be stopped by Skye, only to look down in stunned disbelief and see a knife driven through her heart in the split second before the force animating her dimmed.

Brann stepped in before anyone could stop him. Doing to Lilith what he'd done to Andre, reducing her to skeletal remains so that even with the removal of Skye's blade, she would not live again.

When it was done, silence reigned until the vampire who'd officiated the challenge stepped into the circle and collected the athames. "These deaths are justifiable in accordance with our laws. If you will lift your ward, Brann, then I will see to the disposal of the bodies."

Brann nodded, his low voice barely audible as his chant brought down the barrier keeping them in the room. Then he joined Rafe, his arms going around Syndelle, his hands joining Rafael's as they stroked over Syndelle's naked form, his heart buffeted by a choppy wave of emotion.

He'd thought to possess her, but it was he who was possessed!

Should I replay one of your many lectures about Angelini mates, Sire? Gian asked, his snicker like sandpaper against Brann's nerves.

Would you like to end up in the same condition as Andre and Lilith?

Gian's laugh indicated his lack of fear.

Skye bent down and retrieved Syndelle's clothes. *Leave it to you guys to demand that your companions have to fight to the death naked.*

Blood and death and sex are all closely entwined for us, Gian said, leaning in to kiss his Angelini mate. His erection proving the truth of his words.

The wolf stirred. Now that the danger had passed it wanted to celebrate, it wanted to mate. Syndelle pulled back, her gaze meeting Brann's, then Rafe's, her heart swelling at the pride and love she read in their eyes, her nostrils flaring at the scent of their rising lust.

Syndelle stepped away from them and took her clothes from Skye, hugging her sister, the hum in their blood becoming a roar of love and solidarity so that no words were necessary between them.

"If this is what happens from discovering I've got a sister," Skye teased, "I can hardly wait to see what happens when I meet the rest of the family."

Syndelle laughed. "I think you will find that our brothers are always up for a good hunt. You will fit in well with them."

Rafe grinned then, the last of his fear and guilt fading away. "Ready to blow this joint, babe?" he asked, laughing when her nose wrinkled at his gangster imitation.

She hastily donned her clothes. "More than ready."

Rafael took one of Syndelle's hands. Brann took the other, bringing it to his lips and saying, *You are my life.*

The link shared by just the three of them filled with Syndelle's tender amusement. *As is Rafe,* she reminded, and Brann laughed in response. Parodying her earlier conversation with his often troublesome companion, saying, *As is Rafe. When he's not being a pain in my ass.*

About the Author

ରେ

Jory has been writing since childhood and has never outgrown being a daydreamer. When she's not hunched over her computer, lost in the muse and conjuring up new heroes and heroines, she can usually be found reading, riding her horses, or hiking with her dogs.

Jory welcomes mail from readers. You can write to her c/o Ellora's Cave Publishing at 1056 Home Avenue, Akron OH 44310-3502.

Why an electronic book?

We live in the Information Age — an exciting time in the history of human civilization in which technology rules supreme and continues to progress in leaps and bounds every minute of every hour of every day. For a multitude of reasons, more and more avid literary fans are opting to purchase e-books instead of paperbacks. The question to those not yet initiated to the world of electronic reading is simply: *why?*

1. *Price.* An electronic title at Ellora's Cave Publishing and Cerridwen Press runs anywhere from 40-75% less than the cover price of the <u>exact same title</u> in paperback format. Why? Cold mathematics. It is less expensive to publish an e-book than it is to publish a paperback, so the savings are passed along to the consumer.

2. *Space.* Running out of room to house your paperback books? That is one worry you will never have with electronic novels. For a low one-time cost, you can purchase a handheld computer designed specifically for e-reading purposes. Many e-readers are larger than the average handheld, giving you plenty of screen room. Better yet, hundreds of titles can be stored within your new library — a single microchip. (Please note that Ellora's Cave and Cerridwen Press does not endorse any specific brands. You can check our website at www.ellorascave.com or

www.cerridwenpress.com for customer recommendations we make available to new consumers.)

3. *Mobility.* Because your new library now consists of only a microchip, your entire cache of books can be taken with you wherever you go.

4. *Personal preferences are accounted for.* Are the words you are currently reading too small? Too large? Too…**ANNOYING**? Paperback books cannot be modified according to personal preferences, but e-books can.

5. *Instant gratification.* Is it the middle of the night and all the bookstores are closed? Are you tired of waiting days—sometimes weeks—for online and offline bookstores to ship the novels you bought? Ellora's Cave Publishing sells instantaneous downloads 24 hours a day, 7 days a week, 365 days a year. Our e-book delivery system is 100% automated, meaning your order is filled as soon as you pay for it.

Those are a few of the top reasons why electronic novels are displacing paperbacks for many an avid reader. As always, Ellora's Cave and Cerridwen Press welcomes your questions and comments. We invite you to email us at service@ellorascave.com, service@cerridwenpress.com or write to us directly at: 1056 Home Ave. Akron OH 44310-3502.

THE
☥ ELLORA'S CAVE ☥
LIBRARY

Stay up to date with Ellora's Cave Titles in
Print with our Quarterly Catalog.

TO RECIEVE A CATALOG,
SEND AN EMAIL WITH YOUR NAME
AND MAILING ADDRESS TO:

CATALOG@ELLORASCAVE.COM

OR SEND A LETTER OR POSTCARD
WITH YOUR MAILING ADDRESS TO:

CATALOG REQUEST
c/o ELLORA'S CAVE PUBLISHING, INC.
1056 HOME AVENUE
AKRON, OHIO 44310-3502

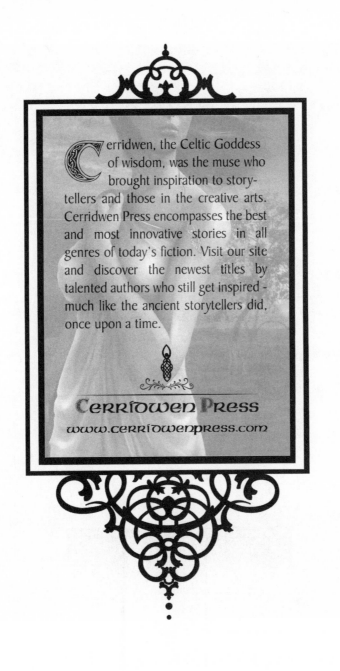

Cerridwen, the Celtic Goddess of wisdom, was the muse who brought inspiration to storytellers and those in the creative arts. Cerridwen Press encompasses the best and most innovative stories in all genres of today's fiction. Visit our site and discover the newest titles by talented authors who still get inspired - much like the ancient storytellers did, once upon a time.

Cerridwen Press

www.cerridwenpress.com